In February, 1955, the Los Angeles Police Department
conducted a contest to create a motto for the Police Academy
"that would express in a few words some or all of the ideals
to which the police service is dedicated."
The winning entry was submitted by officer Joseph S. Dorobeck—

To Protect and Serve

With the passage of time, the motto received wide exposure
and acceptance throughout the Department.
On November 4, 1963, the Los Angeles City Council passed
the necessary ordinance and the motto was adopted
and inscribed on the doors of all LAPD patrol cars,
where it may be seen today.

Also by Roger F. Kennedy

The Windup Man
Lauri with an i
The Three of Us
Mirror Image

*A few of the characters depicted in "Day Watch at Hollywood"
also appear in these four short story collections*

DAY WATCH AT HOLLYWOOD

A CRIME NOVEL

ROGER F. KENNEDY

To order additional copies of this book, contact:
Xlibris Corporation
1-888-795-4274
www.Xlibris.com
Orders@Xlibris.com
86162

Dedication

For Angela and Byron Long

Acknowledgement

*In the creation of this fiction book, I am grateful for
and appreciative of the valuable counsel
and technical assistance of former
Los Angeles Police Department officer Frank Scurria.*

Note

*Los Angeles Police Department
official forms have been modified and abbreviated
for reasons of available space.*

—RFK

DAY WATCH AT HOLLYWOOD

1

The raw metallic sound was part of the whole sorry scene. But today, for the first time, it sounded sweet. The cell door rolled open and Victor Krait stepped into the aisle.

"You're up," Wheelock said to him. "Time to trot."

Wheelock was his jailor, a load of muscled flesh with a bald head and bad teeth, a flunky hardly worth paying attention to. Krait followed him down the cell row. Voices said, "Later, Krait," and "Stay cool, man."

Terminal Island Correctional Institute wasn't the worst of prisons. It was a low-security Federal prison sited on the north end of an island in L. A. Harbor. From the yard the inmates could see sailboats gliding past, free as swans. To the shore side were dozens of harbor cranes and vast parking lots packed with imported cars. At one time or another, T. I. had housed such fabled prisoners as Salvatore Bonanno, G. Gordon Liddy and Timothy Leary.

But all of that was irrelevant to Krait, who silently raged at being deprived of his freedom to work his criminal agenda. Krait was resourceful, however, owing to a strong sense of self-preservation. During his stretch, he was able to generate respect among the more violent inmates by inflating his rap sheet into a major crime wave, leading up to the bank robbery. And then there was Carina Parra. Her frequent visits had kept him from losing sight of the world outside.

At the end of the row he was taken down a stairway to the floor below and through a massive remote-controlled steel door. In the Administration Section, Wheelock turned him over to an officer for processing. He was given his clothes and $50 in small bills. He put on the clothes in a locker room and tossed his jumpsuit into a hamper.

"Keep your nose clean, guy," the officer said. "Don't come back. We hardly have room for the real scum anymore."

"I won't be back, unless it's on a gurney," Krait said. He exited Terminal Island Federal Prison into glorious California sunlight. A few minutes later he boarded an MTD bus bound for Long Beach.

Victor Krait had faced a charge of Federal Bank Robbery, a Class C felony that carried a penalty of twenty to life. With the help of his lawyer, he pled down to grand theft and a rescission of the life term. Time off for good behavior (and a shortage of beds at T.I.) led to his release after twelve years. His partner wasn't so lucky. Raphael Parra had been shot dead by an LAPD cop named Jack Stiles.

Krait remembered it with cinematic clarity. He and Raphael had timed the robbery to occur right after an armored car delivery of neatly bagged cash. No shots were fired and it all looked like roses. They hurried out the back of the bank with Parra carrying the canvas money bag. In the alley leading to the getaway car, Krait tossed his mask into a dumpster.

Then everything went wrong. Two cops happened to be in the area and they spotted the two men running, Parra still wearing his Arnold Schwarzenegger mask. Krait had the getaway car in sight when he was braced by a female cop. The cute little bitch had a gun pointed right between his eyes. A few minutes later Krait heard the shots that killed Parra.

No, I won't be back to Terminal Island, Krait vowed. He'd be more careful this time. He would track down Jack Stiles, the guy who blew up his perfect bank job.

Carina Parra was a true Latin beauty, 5'8," dark-haired and slim.

Her eyes were a clear hazel framed with long lashes. Her seamless skin, which she flaunted constantly, was a subtle shade of cafe au lait. Her breasts, though not large, were perfectly formed. She was a good match for Krait, who was four inches taller. In heels, she could kiss him with scarcely a tilt of her head.

Carina had been only 22 when Raphael Parra was killed. Raph was 35, handsome, strong and passionate. She'd loved him, though he sometimes abused her. In his more gentle moments he could ignite her deepest emotions. She had been with Krait even before Raphael, and knew that he still desired her. She would use that desire for her own purposes.

Carina's current boyfriend, Raymondo, didn't know about Krait. And a good thing too—Raydo would cut Krait's liver out if he knew. It was going to be a high-wire act to sleep with both men, she realized. But maybe there was a way to use Raydo and then get rid of him. Variations on this theme ran through her mind as she drove south on the 710 toward Long Beach.

Krait slid into a booth at a coffee shop along Long Beach Boulevard. He looked out the window at the passing scene. In the early June warmth the girls were showing plenty of skin. He started to feel better than he'd felt in a long time.

Carina walked in a few minutes later, spring fresh in a flower-print sun dress and strap sandals. He gave her a brief hug and kiss.

"You look like a peach sundae," he told her.

She smiled. "And you look like a new man, querida. Prison must've been good for you."

"Educational, let us say. Where did you get that dress?"

"Forever 21. I like their style."

A waitress approached and handed them menus. They ordered white wine.

"So how did it go?" Carina asked.

"As usual, I suppose. They handed me a few bucks and off I went. It was laughable."

"We'll have to do something about those clothes, you know. You want to be more casual, less noticeable."

"I'm sure you have it all scoped out."

"No problem," she shrugged. "But first we need to find a motel."

"Okay, so let's skip the food."

Twenty minutes later they checked into a room at a Garden Inn. Krait hung the Don't Disturb sign on the knob. Leaning against the door inside, he reached for her and the kisses came wet and luscious.

He picked her up and carried her to the bed. "Sorry," he said. "I'm a little pent up."

"Me too, querido. But now the days are long."

Ramondo was suspicious of Carina's stories about Victor Krait. No way did he buy her casual dismissal of his questions. He sat down at her breakfast table and pulled her in as she passed by, tearing the flimsy baby doll she wore.

"Hey, that cost forty bucks," she cried.

"You're fucking that guy Krait, aren't you," he said flat out.

"Of course not, querido."

"Don't lie to me, you stupid bitch." He took a fistful of her hair and tugged. It hurt enough to make her eyes run.

"I'm not. Victor was a friend of my father's. I've known him a long time. He wanted me to pick him up from prison, and I did. That's all. He means nothing to me."

He slapped her face. "I said don't lie to me!"

"Please, Raydo," she wept. "It's not like you think. He wants you to do a job for him."

"What kind of job?"

"It's better if you hear it from him."

"I want to hear it from you." He ripped the baby doll to shreds, leaving her naked and afraid. "Get down on your knees, bitch."

She sank, thinking fast. "All right. He wants you to kill Jack Stiles. He'll pay you more than you could dream of."

Fortunately for Carina, money was the one thing that could soothe Raydo.

At this time Krait was busy elsewhere. With money he borrowed from Carina, he bought a gun off the street. It wasn't too difficult to locate a source. He simply began asking around in East Hollywood, where the Latino gangs were. It wasn't long before a local arms dealer opened the trunk of his sedan to show him a number of weapons ranging from small caliber semi-automatics to sawed-off shotguns. Krait's choice was a Smith and Wesson pistol with a threaded barrel, and a silencer to go with it. The combination would serve his purpose perfectly.

Jack Stiles and Traci Little were detectives working out of LAPD Hollywood Division. Officially ID'd as a single unit, they were the most intuitive pair that Lieutenant John Luttwak ever had on his Homicide squad.

Stiles had been a tight end in college and at the age of 38 he hadn't lost a step. His BMI was a perfect 22.5. He'd come up from the ranks after eight years of patrol duty. He was a tough and resourceful detective, respected by everyone at the station. When the chips were down, they knew Stiles would be there.

Traci Little started as a patrol officer. She was a quick study and rapidly acquired a raft of street smarts. Her experience on the streets was key to her rapid ascent. At 29, she advanced to D-I homicide detective and quickly fit in. She also happened to be grade A sexy—5'8," with coyote blond hair, almond eyes, and a yard of great legs. Around the detectives bullpen she wore slim black jeans and low heels. In the field she wore Nikes. Off duty she couldn't slip into a short skirt fast enough.

The other thing about Stiles and Traci was that they were deep into sex—not just tension relief, but a true and faithful relationship. This required a great deal of discretion. There could be no lingering glances in the squad room, no embraces in the parking lot. When they went to The Full Clip for drinks they took care to arrive and leave separately. Nevertheless, Luttwak wondered.

One morning after roll call he called Stiles into his cluttered office, a partitioned area in a corner of the squad room. He motioned him to one of his two draw-up chairs.

"Everything going okay, Jack?" he said.

"Sure," Stiles said. "Is there a problem?"

Luttwak fiddled with his pen, clearly uncomfortable. "I want to ask you something flat out. Are you and Traci, shall we say, emotionally involved?"

"That depends on what emotional means. I would take a bullet for her, and she'd do the same for me."

"Let me put it this way. I don't know if you're seeing her, but if you are there can be serious consequences. If sex is involved, one of you would have to be transferred to another division. And I would lose my best homicide team."

"I'm aware of that, Lieutenant."

Luttwak stood up.

"Take care, Jack. Keep your eye on the job."

"Trust me, I will."

Stiles left the office feeling a little iffy. He hadn't lied, yet he hadn't exactly been forthcoming either.

2

No one knew about Krait's numbered account in Zurich, not even Carina. He kept the number, one digit shy of a palindrome, saved in his head. He needed several thousand dollars to work with. The trouble was, he had no local bank to wire it to. In order to open an account he needed a new identity. Clyde Crawley was his man.

Crawley still lived in the same house in Hollywood that Krait had recalled. Not much had changed, just gotten older and shabbier. It was an old 1930s California bungalow with a front porch and gray asphalt tiles on the roof. Half-dead geraniums flanked the steps. A kinked hose lay curled near its bib like a dead snake.

Krait knocked on the door, wondering if he would be disappointed. But no, the door opened and there stood an older version of the Crawley he'd remembered. He still looked like nobody you'd care to know. He had the same bald top with same frowsy hair around the sides, almost white now.

Crawley removed his magnifying spectacles and peered at Krait.

"My stars, if it ain't Victor. How long has it been, amigo?"

"Ten or twelve years," Krait said. "I wasn't actually sure I'd find you."

"Well, y'did. Come on in."

Crawley led the way back to his workshop, which was two bedrooms with the wall knocked out. Tables were filled with tools, materials, old TVs and computers and parts of them. Wall shelves contained lesser items, even old shellac singles of Benny Goodman and Artie Shaw.

He pulled a canvas director's chair up to the workbench for Krait. On the bench, a 27" iMac was dimmed and would soon go to sleep. There were engraving tools and a big repro camera for making litho plates, and stacks of various paper stocks and plastic sheets.

"So what brings you here, Victor?" Crawley said. "Up to no good, I'll wager."

"Just a simple job you could do in your sleep," Krait said. "I need a new identity that I can use to open an account at a bank. Social Security card, driver's license, a couple of credit cards, you know the drill."

"It'll cost you, you know. Things ain't the way they used to be."

"No doubt. When can I pick up the work?"

"Friday. A thousand ought to cover it. Just tell me who you want to be."

Krait thought it over for a moment. "How about Guy X. Terminus?"

"You got it, amigo."

Krait stayed long enough to have his photo taken. He knew Crawley would delete the image when he was through with it.

John Luttwak was feeling like a new man these days. He faced his work with renewed energy and sense of purpose. The main cause of his renaissance was Diane Metz, a psychologist with the LAPD Behavioral Sciences Division. He'd known Diane for a few years in the course of various investigations. As a PhD in cognitive science, she'd provided key testimony in court on some of his toughest cases.

Luttwak's then wife, Celine, had become increasingly tired of his chosen field of work. She found law enforcement to be toxic to any human relationship. To her, it felt like being shackled to an ugly and depressing Job. She hated his favorite bar, The Full Clip, and all the drinking and the cop talk.

Celine began to spend less and less of her time at home, in favor of more time out with "the girls." The situation finally came to a breaking point when one night he failed to check with her from The Full Clip. A fight ensued, an unforgiving one that neither really intended.

The next morning Celine asked him for a divorce. It was a shock to Luttwak, who wanted to save the marriage, if only for the sakes of their two children and a grandson. He resisted the divorce to the extent that he could, but in the end he had to grant her wishes. It made him feel culpable, both for being the cause of it and for the granting of it. With a silent house and no one to share it with, he spent most of his time at work or at The Clip with his friends and fellow cops. He became what she accused him of—married to the Job.

One day at Hollywood station, Luttwak encountered Diane Metz coming down the stairway from the second floor. They exchanged greetings and minor catch-up talk. Aware of his current situation, Diane asked him to have a drink with her, no strings attached. Pleased and at loose ends, he accepted her offer.

Luttwak had always liked Diane. In the course of his work he'd always thought of her as a talented professional, but never as a romantic interest. To his amazement, the blue-eyed business-like psychologist turned out to be warm and sexy. After drinks and dinner at Larchmont Grill, she asked him in for a nightcap.

Diane's apartment was modest but welcoming in its feminine furnishings—Good art, abundant books, off-white seating with colorful throw pillows, 3-inch white shutters.

Sipping sherry out of small tumblers, they lounged on her sofa debating the merits of intellectual British mystery novels versus the tougher American crime books. Diane liked the intricately plotted puzzles of Agatha Christie, G. K. Chesterton, Dorothy L. Sayers, and currently, Martha Grimes. Luttwak preferred the more hard-boiled works of Hammett, Chandler and McBain.

Diane brought her legs up side-saddle to him, with her skirt ooching up in the process. Within Luttwak, emotions long buried stirred. He reached for her and they kissed, tentatively at first, then with depth and passion. "No strings" turned out to be the beginning of a full-blown love affair.

Next month at The Full Clip they would celebrate the first anniversary of their marriage.

3

Victor Krait picked up his phony documents on Friday afternoon. Crawley swept the trash off his work table and spread them out. They all had yellowed paper and worn edges to make them look used.

"Well, what do y'think?" Crawley said.

"They're perfect," Krait said, for once truthfully.

"You won't have a bit of trouble with these, Victor. They're worth every dollar of that twelve hundred."

"You said a grand."

"Well, I had to work a couple of nights on this job."

"It's a moot point."

"That's right. These docs are absolutely untraceable."

"I'm sure." Krait opened his briefcase and pulled out the Smith and Wesson pistol, a round already chambered, and began screwing on the silencer.

Crawley's eyes got big and he wet his lips. "Don't do this, amigo. Let's negotiate. I'm sure we can work a deal."

"Relax. You think I'd actually shoot you?" Krait said.

"You're just scaring me, right? You wouldn't kill an old friend."

"Friend? Don't be absurd." He chugged two rounds into Crawley's head. Blood and small globby shreds sprayed the wall behind him.

"Have a nice trip, amigo."

Krait gathered up the forgeries and placed them in his briefcase. The still hot pistol went into a separate compartment. He wiped down everything he might have touched. Last thing, he opened the back of Crawley's computer and removed the hard drive.

Jack Stiles was a self-contained man. Like many unmarried cops, he had few personal possessions. He lived in a one bedroom apartment that he spent little time in. The place came with maple furniture and cheap seascapes. Stiles was not well read, although his mind was clear and capable. His one bookcase held a few cheap paperbacks, mainly by Robert Crais and Carl Hiaasen, and a couple of gun manuals and a stack of ballistic reports. In a corner was a 36-inch flat screen TV on a stand. Where most people had comfy chairs, Stiles had a Bowflex home gym.

In the tiny kitchen there was a fridge, mostly for breakfast juice and fruit, and a combination range and oven that he rarely used. On the counter, a toaster, a plug-in coffee maker and a microwave oven. As for computing, he deferred to the LAPD standard issue PC on his desk at work.

Three nights a week Stiles ate bar food at The Full Clip. At home, he liked to watch classic cop movies, like "Bullett" and "Magnum Force." He loved the highjacking scene at SFO where Inspector Callahan says, "May I make a suggestion?" In the next cut Callahan is boarding the plane dressed in a pilot's uniform. Then he's in the cockpit trying to taxi the big jet to the takeoff line. Needless to say he messes up the hijackers, killing one with his long barrel Magnum.

Sometimes old friends from the Academy would come over for beer and hot dogs and a Dodger game. That was fun but hardly a social life. Mostly, he'd rather be someplace else. When boredom became intolerable he would go to Traci's condo. She would stoke up his fire in a hurry.

Crawley's landlord, J. B. Owens, was worried about him. Owens frequently chewed the fat with Crawley, mainly about horse racing, odds and betting. He hadn't seen Crawley for several days and wondered if something bad had happened to him. He noticed that the outdoor lights were on and the geraniums were dry. That wasn't like Clyde. He finally decided to called the police.

Car 6A55 was dispatched to the location to check it out. Patrol Officer Rick Onofre met with Owens on Crawley's front porch. "Unlock the door but don't open it," Onofre said to him. "I'll go in and have a look around."

Onofre quickly discovered Crawley's body in his workshop lying in a patch of dried blood. With no weapon in sight, he knew he was looking at a homicide. He drew his service weapon and walked through the house to make sure the shooter wasn't still present and there were no other dead or injured. Outside, he locked the door and extracted the key. He told Owens that Crawley was dead, and that he was declaring the house a crime scene.

"I'll keep the key. No one is to enter, not even you, capisce?" He went to his car and reported to his RTO: Location, suspected homicide, shed blood, request backup and paramedics. The premises were soon swarming with LAPD cops.

Two patrol units responded to secure the area. A crime scene Field Team arrived and began the process of gathering evidence. Photographs were taken. Ballistic materials were picked up or dug out. Samples of blood and tissue were scraped from the body, floor and walls. Samples of inks, dyes and paper stock were placed in bags and held for evidence. Later the coroner's van arrived to deal with Crawley's remains. All physical evidence was sent to the LAPD Forensic Analysis Section.

Onofre filled out the first of many reports:

LOS ANGELES POLICE DEPARTMENT
INVESTIGATIVE REPORT

CASE SCREENING FACTOR(S)	REPORT OF:	DIV	INC #	DR #
SUSPECT VEHICLE NOT SEEN	*HOMICIDE*	*HWD*	*7754*	*20II-06-7754*

	REPORTING PERS.	LAST NAME	FIRST NAME	M.I.
__M.O. NOT DISTINCT		*OWENS*	*JAMES*	*S*
PRINTS, OTHER EVIDENCE NOT AVAIL.				

ADDRESS	ZIP	PHONE
1680 N. WHITLEY AVE	*90028*	*323-113-902*

DRIVER'S LIC #	FOREIGN LANG	OCCUPATION
Z0572255	*NO*	*ACCOUNTANT*

PREMISES TYPE OF	LOCATION OF OCCURRENCE	RES	BUS	DATE	TIME
SING FAM HOME	*1905 SERRANO ST—HWD*	*X*		*6-23-11*	*0630 HRS*

ENTRY POINT OF ENTRY	POINT OF EXIT	INSTRUMENT USED
FRONT DOOR	*SAME*	*NO FORCEFUL ENTRY*

VICT. VEHICLE YEAR, MAKE, MODEL	PROPERTY STOLEN / DAMAGED	$ AMT.
90'S TOYOTA CORO (NOT INVOLVED)	*PRINTED (FALSE) DOCUMENTS*	*??*

M.O. IN BRIEF PHRASES DESCRIBE SUSPECT'S ACTIONS, INCLUDING WEAPON USED. IF ANY MISSING ITEMS ARE POTENTIALLY IDENTIFIABLE, ITEMIZE AND DESCRIBE.IN THIS INCIDENT NARRATIVE.

SUSPECT ENTERED FR DOOR, SHOT VICT WITH 9MM SEMI-AUTOMATIC FIREARM, 2 ROUNDS TO THE HEAD, KILLING HIM. SUSP RANSACKED PREMISES FOR DOCUMENTS, REMOVED PC HARD DRIVE. DEPARTED UNK DIRECTION.

SUSPECT 1: NAME	ADDRESS	CITY	ZIP	BKG #	CHARGE
	— UNKNOWN —				

DESCRIPTION; HAIR, EYES, HEIGHT, WEIGHT, AGE, CLOTHING PERSONAL ODDITIES (SCARS, TATTOOS)
WEAPON: (VERBAL THREATS, BODILY FORCE, SIMULATED GUN, ETC. IF KNIFE OR GUN, DESCRIBE FULLY,

SUSPECT 2: NAME	ADDRESS	CITY	ZIP	BKG #	CHARGE
	— UNKNOWN, IF ANY—				

DESCRIPTION; HAIR, EYES, HEIGHT, WEIGHT, AGE, CLOTHING PERSONAL ODDITIES (SCARS, TATTOOS)
WEAPON: VERBAL THREATS, BODILY FORCE, SIMULATED GUN, ETC. IF KNIFE OR GUN, DESCRIBE FULLY,

SUSPECT VEHICLE (IF INVOLVED)	— NOT INVOLVED —			
YEAR, MAKE,	MODEL,	COLOR,	LICENSE NO.	STATE
INTERIOR	BODY	WINDOWS	ACCESSORIES	
__BUCKET SEATS	__DAMAGED	__DAMAGED	__SATELLITE NAV	
__LEATHER	__RUST, PRIMER	__SMOKED	__STEREO __CD	__DVD

REPORTING OFFICER

INITIAL, LAST NAME *R. ONOFRE* SERIAL NO. *7075524* DIV. *HWD* SIGNATURE *Rick Onofre*

4

0600 hours marked the start of the 12-hour day watch at Hollywood station. Lieutenant John Luttwak called two of his homicide teams into his corner cubicle. Once the door closed, the hustle-bustle of the squad room outside softened and the lighting was less glaring.

The cubicle was a working office. Two-drawer file cabinets were lined up along one wall, topped by stacks of cases, open and closed. Shelves above contained manuals, a cork board with current bulletins, mug shots and street maps, and a well worn copy of the LAPD Manual of Operations. Family pictures of Luttwak's children from his former marriage rested on his desk, along with a picture of Luttwak and Diane Metz in Hawaii with leis around their necks. On top of a stack of current cases, an LAPD Mounted Police belt buckle served as a paperweight.

Two detective teams were present—Jack Stiles and Traci Little, and Dick Cheevers and Ed Chase. These two teams were next up on the lieutenant's homicide investigative assignment list. The detectives drew chairs up to a conference table with their laptops and notepads.

Luttwak passed out an Open Case file containing the latest evidence in the Clyde Crawley case. Its DR number, 2011-06-7754 indicated that it was the 7,754th incident at Hollywood Division so far that year.

"Jack and Traci, you're up for this case," Luttwak said. "Dick and Ed, I want you to sit in just for your info. This is chapter and verse on Crawley. If you need to refer to it in the field, you'll find it in your laptop."

The detectives thumbed through the printed sheets.

"Sorry 'bout Clyde," Cheevers said. "He was a nice old dude, in spite of his trade." Cheevers was black, and built like an NBA power forward. As strong as Stiles was, Dick could beat him two-to-one in arm wrestling. In temperament, Dick was more easygoing than his thin-lipped partner Ed Chase or hard-ass Kazurian, another of the detectives. No way did it make him any the less effective.

"There wasn't a better paper man in town than Crawley," he said.

"Yeah. Tell the Feds about it," Chase said.

Turning the pages, Stiles said, "Another cheap semi-auto, serial number filed off. The weapon of choice on the street these days. Field unit dug two 9mm slugs out of the wall. The brass was lying on the floor."

"Firearms Unit sent images to NIBIN yesterday," Luttwak said. "Nothing as yet." NIBIN was National Integrated Ballistics Information Network.

"There's no help from fingerprints," Traci noted. "There's just Crawley's."

"The shooter wasn't that stupid," Cheevers said.

Luttwak played with his pen. "That's a lot of 'no's so far." He turned to Stiles. "Jack, you and Traci jump all over this one. See if anybody is singing about Crawley."

"If not, we'll hum a few bars," Traci said.

"Dick, you and Ed are next up. I want you to cover that celebrity shooting last night. Get after the boyfriend."

"Right."

Stiles said, "I'd like to take a closer look at the Crawley evidence. I'm talking about the actual paper. Not that I don't love these leaky inkjet copies."

"Whatever," Luttwak said. "It's all downtown at Property Division, awaiting your eager clutches." He rose and gathered up some binders. "I have to duck out. I've got a meeting with Captain McKnight."

The Captain, commonly referred to as Uptight McKnight, was a paper pusher who supervised Luttwak and others in the squad room. He was disliked and ignored by just about every cop in the Division.

"My sympathies, boss," Cheevers said as Luttwak walked out.

Traci Little awakened as usual at five o'clock, with the early light just beginning to slant into her third story condo. First things first, she peed and took a shower. Next she pulled on her bikini briefs and started the coffee.

Traci was a born and bred earth girl. She was pleased with the body God gave her and wasn't shy about showing it off. As a college senior, Traci waited tables and earned enough to rent a tiny apartment. In the warmer months, she would spend much of her private time topless. She liked the feeling of air on her skin, it was that simple.

Traci didn't have a Bowflex gym like Stiles did, but she kept her body well toned. She was strong enough to bring down a good-sized man before he knew the way to San Jose. Some of this was the result of her Academy training, but most of it was due to the aerobics routine she did every day, rain or shine.

Traci's mother died at the age of 35 after a long struggle with lung cancer, still begging for a smoke in her final hours. One would think it more likely that her father, a Culver City fireman, would be the one whose lungs would fail, but that's not the way life works. It was a struggle for Stephen Little, but he raised Traci and Liz by himself and enrolled them at UCLA. He was surprised when Traci expressed an interest in law enforcement. Five years later he died in a collapsed building. It was only two weeks after watching her graduate from the Police Academy.

Traci padded onto her balcony and leaned over the rail. Below she could see her 75-year-old building manager raking some leaves. She depended on Nathan and liked to give him a cheap thrill every so often.

She waved at him. "Hi, Nathan, how you doing today?"

"Terrific so far, PD girl," he waved back.

Nathan would do anything for Traci, including giving her a key to the roof. He knew she liked to go up there and work on her seamless tan. Nate also showed her where the back door key was staked out.

Time to go. She put on black stretch jeans and a white fleece top, grabbed her kit, and headed for the street level parking area where she kept her cobalt blue Audi roadster. She drove with her Nikes, switched to 2-inch heels at Hollywood station, and back to Nikes in the field.

5

The Full Clip was located on Sunset Boulevard near Alvarado. It was frequented mainly by cops from Hollywood and Rampart Divisions, along with forensic specialists, prosecutors, defense attorneys, federal agents from the local field office and so on. The interior was walnut with brass fixtures and cop memorabilia displayed everywhere. Drinks were toted by cute girls in shorts and Metro T-shirts.

This merciful Friday night, Traci was there in a date dress flimsy enough to make a grown man weep. She sat on a bar stool talking to a couple of P/Os she new from earlier days. They were drinking beer. She nursed a chardonnay.

"How's life on the Detective table, Traci?" Cal Travis said to her.

"Not bad. They have real coffee in the break room."

"Outstanding. Coffee at the fast food joints is so bad I switched to Red Bull."

Travis' partner was Don Anders. He looked Traci up and down and said, "Are you lookin' good or what."

She rolled her eyes. "Being born blond never hurts."

"You were a savvy cop, too," Anders said. "I'm thinking back when you were RTO. How'd you get that job anyway?"

"Right place, right time."

"Don't believe her," Travis told Anders. "She earned it."

"One thing I'll tell you," Traci said. "I earned a first hand picture of what cops face on the street."

"Yeah, stuff happens when you least expect it."

"That's true enough. So what are you two getting up to these days?"

"We're working Special Problems Unit," Travis said. "Mainly busting ticket scalpers at Dodger Stadium."

"How does that go?"

"Well, most scalpers don't have the tickets on them. They're always stashed someplace, like the base of a tree or in some bushes. We spot these guys hanging around the gate. We ask them what they're doing, and they say waiting for a friend or something like that."

"Sometimes the tickets are in plain view," Anders said. "We ask them, are these yours? They say oh no, not ours. So we take the tickets and give them to some kids and tell them they're a gift from the LAPD."

"I love it," Traci said, taking a sip.

At that moment Stiles walked in. He'd spotted Traci's Audi parked in the lot outside.

"Hey, Jack, over here," Travis said, motioning. "Where you keepin' yourself these days?"

"In the back room at Hollywood. And you?"

"Working Dodger Stadium. We were just telling Traci about it."

"So I see." He signaled for a Sam Adams. To Traci, "Are these guys giving you a hard time, partner?"

"Not more than the usual," she said.

Anders resumed. "A lot of these mopes hang around the parking lot, breaking into cars. We're on foot, but we have cops on Elysian Park hill spotting them with binoculars. With our Rovers it's easy to talk back and forth and catch these guys in the act. We carry the Rovers in paper bags like winos with booze."

"I always wondered about you two," Traci said.

By this time The Clip was filled with LAPD cops, wives, girlfriends, forensic techs, lawyers, and staffers. Norm Nomura from the Medical Examiner's office stopped by.

"Pull up a stool, Norm," Stiles said. "How's your pals, the walking dead?"

"They're all at the studios making vampire movies."

"Please, you're creeping me out," Traci said.

Nomura told an old joke about three zombies at the Pearly Gates. St. Peter asked the first zombie, "What did you do in life?" "I staggered a lot, and drooled," the zombie replied. "You go to the bad place," St. Peter said. The second zombie answered, "I drank blood." St. Peter said, "You go to the bad place." St. Peter turned to the third zombie. "And what did you do in life?" The zombie answered, "I ate a lawyer." St. Peter said, "You can come in." Laughter and hoots burst out.

Next was Larry the Cable Guy's line, What happens if you're scared half to death twice? And so on into the night.

Stiles and Traci left at different times.

Krait stowed his fake Social Security card and Drivers License in his wallet. The second step in his new identity plan was to open a checking account. This he accomplished at First Hollywood Bank, close to Carina's house. A pleasant young woman with dark eyes and a corkscrew hair-do handled the paper work.

"I'll just open with twenty dollars for now," he told her. "Tomorrow I'm expecting a large deposit by wire."

"Very good," she said. "Is there anything else I can help you with, Mr. Terminus? Safe deposit box, perhaps? Car financing?"

"Yes, but not until I get settled." In truth he'd love to have a decent car. Borrowing Carina's Corolla was awkward and public transit was the pits. He seethed at the thought that Stiles and his sexpot partner we're the cause of his humiliation.

Krait's father had been a mentalist. In this persona he'd encountered many gullible rich women who were willing to believe anything.

In private sessions Manfred Krait would hypnotize them, kiss them and fondle them and tell them they would awaken completely fulfilled. With increasing success he became more and more daring, until one day one of his subjects found teeth marks on her nipples. Manfred's next client turned out to be an LAPD Sex Detective. His lawyer pleaded him to 18 months and probation. After that he went back to just cheating at cards.

Victor had never forgotten his father's advice: "Never lift a woman's skirt unless you're sure of her." Well he had no worries about Carina. After Raydo's rapacious style, she was primed for a lifetime of exhilarating sex with him.

6

The LAPD Administration Building downtown housed the Property Division, a huge repository containing physical evidence from thousands of crimes. Much of it had been logged into computers, but not the most recent cases. The property check-out window was the venue of Steve Wolfe, a nose guard-sized clerk Stiles knew from earlier days.

"Jack, you rascal," Wolfe said. "It's been a while, hasn't it."

"Too true. This is my partner, Traci Little."

"Nice to meet you, Traci. Jack and I were at the Academy together. I dropped out and ended up here."

"Hi, Steve. Happy to know you."

"So what brings you two to my humble window?"

"We're working the Crawley murder," Stiles said. "Lieutenant Luttwak wants us to review the CS materials." He turned over the paperwork.

"That's fairly fresh. Hang on."

In a few minutes, Wolfe returned with two sealed boxes. Attached was a property log in a clear folder. Stiles signed and dated the log.

"Jack, who you got in the Lakers-Cleveland game?" Wolfe asked.

"Twenty bucks worth of Lakers."

"Don't be too sure. Take care, you guys."

In the adjoining anteroom, the two detectives laid out the proceeds on a conference table. The smaller box contained envelopes, each signed by a Field Unit specialist. One of the envelopes contained 4x6 photographic prints, marked with a number keyed to a diagram of the scene. Two more contained the slugs and brass, macro photos of each, and a report from NIBIN, the FBI's National Integrated Ballistics Information site, stating that the gun had been used in other crimes and passed hand-to-hand on the street.

"The gun has been around the block, I see," Stiles said.

"No surprise, considering Crawley's clientele."

Other envelopes included lab analyses of stains and fluids, adhesives and glues, and samples of various inks and paper stocks, some of it U. S. banknote paper.

"Here's the dye and chemical test results. Mostly used to make drivers' licenses and passports. Blood stains all belong to Crawley. These other marks are unidentified."

"Where's the computer?"

It was in the second box, along with a large number of CD-Rs.

"The killer was no goofball. He removed the hard drive."

Stiles picked up an envelope full of CD-Rs and read the summary. "Shit, these are all dupes of country music albums."

Traci laughed. "I'm starting to like this old guy."

"You know, some of this stuff might actually be useful if we ever get a suspect."

"Here's what we're after, Jack. Some reject Social Security proofs. They're smeared or flawed in one way or another."

Stiles dealt them right side up like the flop in Texas hold'em. Edwin Smith, James R. Johnson, Willard Peterson, Vincent Baker, Sharon Jones, Guy X. Terminus . . .

Traci looked them over. "One of these dudes got pissed at Crawley's choice of names and blew him away."

"I guess. People have killed for less than that."

Carina managed to find an open afternoon to meet with Victor Krait. The place was a Starbucks near McArthur park that offered an angled view of the lake. Krait walked in, looking like a blue-eyed version of Jeremy Irons. He spotted Carina sitting by a window in a bare summer dress.

"You're my strawberry ice cream dessert," he said to her.

"Thank you, querido. You are very handsome yourself."

"I finally found time to buy some decent clothes," he said. "It makes me feel alive."

"Not like a convict waking up to a horn blast everyday."

"No, not ever again. I have great plans for us, my dear. First of all, I'm going to buy a car. No more bumming off of you."

"Really, what kind?"

"I don't know. Something reliable, to be replaced later by a car that you would look lovely in."

"How sweet."

"More important, I've come up with a plan to kill the man who stole twelve years of my life. I propose to offer ten thousand dollars to Raymondo to kill Jack Stiles. Five thousand up front. And the best part is, we'll nail Raydo with the crime."

"But where are you going to get that kind of money?"

"From Zurich, where it awaits me, and you."

Carina put her hands on his. "You amaze me, querido, with your ideas and your resources. I can't wait to be yours alone."

He rose. "I'll fetch us some coffee. How about a latte?"

"Yes, please."

Fetch? she mused. Such a refined word. My life with Victor will be filled with such elegances.

Raydo was excited. "Ten thousand dollars," he laughed. "Shit, I would do it for five hundred. What zonzos these Anglos are."

Visions of new clothes, a convertible, plenty of crystal meth, and Carina with earrings flitted through his mind.

He seized a bottle of Chianti. "Let's celebrate!"

"Not till the deed is done," Carina said.

"You don't doubt me, do you?" He took out his hunting knife and thumbed the blade.

"Not with that, amador. It must be untraceable."

He brightened. "I know the perfect way. Topo will provide me with what I need."

Jack Stiles rolled out of bed at 0515 hours. This was not one of the occasional wake-ups he shared with Traci. No warm and breathing partner next to him with her arm across his chest. No kisses, no luscious female skin.

He turned on the plug-in coffee maker, worked ten minutes on the Bowflex and showered. Stiles' breakfast was healthy, comparatively speaking. This morning he found a brown-spotted banana in the fridge and ate it. Then a blob of no-fat yogurt with apple juice and oat granola mixed in. By this time the coffee was ready, so he drank that while watching CNN. He washed his few dishes the fast and easy way. Scrape, hot water rinse, stack in a drainer.

Preferring a day-old look, Stiles brushed his face only lightly with his shaver. His hair was brown and fairly full, because Traci liked it that way.

As for clothing, his style was no style. He wore what most detectives wore—khaki pants, short sleeve shirt with tie, and one of two sports jackets. Except for court appearances, he ditched the tie as soon as he was clear of the station. Off duty he went with whatever was comfortable, usually a T-shirt and jeans or shorts, and Nikes. He also owned two track jackets, one Raiders and one Steelers, not that he cared about either team.

It was almost time for work, and Stiles didn't want to be late. He strapped on his belt and checked the Baretta 92 he carried on his right hip. His cell phone fit into a pod on the other side. On the back of the belt, his badge and wallet ID, and a set of handcuffs. In his left pocket, two extra magazines for the Baretta. So armed, he shrugged into a jacket, locked up and left.

7

In the busy Hollywood station squad room, Jack Stiles stared at the list of flawed Social Security card proofs in front of him. Traci parked on the corner of his desk with her copy of the list. There were 32 names.

Stiles shook his head. "I have no clue what we can get from these names. The FBI Criminal Database won't have anything real. The names are all fakes."

"We might turn up a couple of pig farmers in Kansas," Traci said.

"Right. And the Social Security numbers won't help us. Even babies have one of those."

"Millions of people have Social Security taxes withheld at work."

"I wouldn't know. My paycheck is always direct deposited at the bank."

"Which you spend on wine and loose women."

Cheevers was passing by. Traci flagged him down. "Dick, are you clued about fake identities?"

"It's a big bucket of worms, but you already know that."

"What's the first thing a guy with a fake Social Security number would do?"

"Get a credit card, then go on a spree."

"Thanks, hon," Traci said.

Cheevers headed for the back door, humming "Fly Me to the Moon."

"A spree, the man says. A new car maybe?" Stiles said.

"It wouldn't be discovered until the first billing period," Traci said.

"How true."

That's a lead they would follow up on. For right now, there was something lurking in those names.

2030 hours, Stiles showed up at Traci's third story condo.

"Detective," she said. "Is this an official call?"

"No, it's a need to be with you call. I'm weary from all the work stuff."

"She gave him a hug and a kiss. "I can fix that, you know."

"Angel of mercy."

"You didn't park out front, did you?"

"No, down the street."

"Sorry to fuss," she sighed. "The thought of those anal retentive I-A cops finding out about us is scary."

"I think maybe Wak suspects, but I doubt if he would turn us in. The man is no snitch."

She released him. "How about some wine? Red or white."

"What color red is it?"

"The cheap kind."

Traci walked to her mini-bar and came up with a bottle of Zinfandel. She poured two glasses and the mood turned more cheerful. She turned on the TV and found Woody Allen on AMC, hyperventilating his way through "Sleeper."

"This movie is so fun," she said. "Let's get better acquainted." This was Traci's code for getting naked.

Minutes later they were snuggling on the sofa like naughty teenagers. By the time the dictator's ear was flattened by the steamroller, they were asleep.

In the morning Stiles awoke with Traci kneeling next to him, with the early light slanting across her body.

"What a piece of God's work you are," he said, shaking his head.

Traci laughed. "You should talk. What about last night when you fell asleep on me?"

"Sorry. Just weary, I guess."

She gave him a tasty orange-flavored kiss, taking her sweet time about it.

"Well, you're up for it now," she said.

Raymondo put the word out on the street. Nothing happened the first day. The second day he was stuffing himself at the local Taqueria when a man sat down at his table. He was a big man, dark-skinned like Raydo.

"You are the one who wishes to see Topo?" the man said.

"Yes."

"About what?"

"The tools to kill a man."

"Come with me." He followed the man to a black sedan.

Federico Cruz, street name "Topo," was well known in the barrios. He was ruthless gangster and drug lord, and a founding member of Florencia 13. The only reason he wasn't in prison was because of the threat of death to anyone who might testify against him. Physically he was a heavy man with a droopy mustache and bad teeth.

An old Hollywood hacienda served Topo as both residence and office. He leaned back in his brass-studded executive chair and appraised Raymondo, who was left standing. A worthless cholo, Topo decided.

"What can I do for you, amigo?" he rasped.

A chill ran through Raydo. This was no time for small talk. "I have to kill a man, but not with a gun or knife."

"I see. What do you need?"

Raydo's heart was racing. "A small cake of C-4. Enough to blow up a car. And also a blasting cap."

"C-4 is very powerful, amigo," Topo said. "A small cake is enough to wipe out half a block."

"I must be sure."

"And who is this enemy you wish to destroy?"

"He is a policeman. A detective who kills our people."

Topo was pleased to hear this. "The cost will be five thousand in cash. Up front."

"That may take me a day or two, patrón."

"Very well. See that this killing does not come back to me. If it does, we will cut your heart out and feed it to you."

In the black sedan again, Raydo felt a surge of supreme confidence. This cop Stiles was as good as dead.

Krait checked his First Hollywood balance by telephone and saw that the wire deposit from his Zurich stash had been credited to his account. He returned to the bank and was again served by the woman with the smoky eyes and the corkscrew hair. She remembered his cool Jeremy Irons looks.

"Nice to see you, Mr. Terminus. How can I help you?"

"I'm going to be visiting an Indian casino near San Diego," he said. "I need to withdraw twenty thousand dollars in fifty- and one hundred-dollar bills."

"Certainly, sir," she smiled. "There's a two-day wait for the withdrawal of large amounts of cash. The truck is due Wednesday at one o'clock. I can have it for you then."

"I see. And for the present?"

"I can release one thousand."

"Let's do that. I'll be back Wednesday for the balance."

"That will be fine. Now I'll go to the vault and be back in a jiffy."

In five minutes by his watch, she was counting out the bills front side up on the counter. "Would you like a container for that, Mr. Terminus?"

"Indeed I would."

She put the bills in a #10 envelope together with a receipt showing the transaction.

Krait walked to Carina's car and tossed it into the glove box. What a bother, he thought. These stupid banks.

8

Wednesday evening, Carina separated the five thousand that would be Raymondo's up front pay, and stashed the rest in a half empty flour canister in her pantry. The second installment was promised when Jack Stiles was dead. According to Krait's plan, Raydo would never see it. Most, if not all, the money would be recovered and Raydo would be disposed of. She didn't know how Victor would do the disposing, but knowing him, it surely would be swift and efficient.

She put on a terry robe and poured herself a glass of Merlot. She turned on a Spanish channel. Edith Marquez was singing one of her favorites, "Acariciame." She began to dance, holding the wine glass in her hand.

She heard the slam of a door and Raymondo appeared, flushed with his successful meeting with Topo.

"It's going to happen," he crowed. "I have arranged for the weapon. The fascist cop will soon be dead!"

"Very good, and I have the money for you. It's here in this envelope."

Raydo seized it and counted the hundred dollar bills. "That Krait. You didn't fuck him for this, did you?"

"Of course not. I told you, he's nothing to me, just an older man who wants to see Jack Stiles dead."

"Be careful." He dragged Carina to her wardrobe mirror and twisted her arms behind her and said, "If I catch you in bed with him, there will be blood on the sheets. Comprende?"

"Por suquesto, amador."

Carina spent the rest of the evening having unfulfilling sex with Raymondo. Her thoughts were elsewhere with Victor.

Stiles pulled out the list of flawed Social Security card names. He sensed there was something there playing peekaboo with him. No law enforcement data base could reveal it—the names were of people that did not exist.

He tried to imagine the state of mind of the killer. He ruled out robbery. Money was still in the desk. This murder had to do with the IDs and/or Crawley himself.

From Stiles' experience, the cleverest of criminals often had inflated egos. They enjoyed tormenting their pursuers, often risking the loss of control of their game. And that could be the key to their identity and arrest.

Across the busy squad room, he saw Traci winding up a cell call. He motioned to her to come over.

"Take another trip through these names, partner. What stands out, if anything?"

Traci looked over his shoulder. She saw what he saw.

"The names are common. That's to be expected, I suppose. Most fugitives would choose a name that was the same as a lot of other people's."

"Ah, the old hide-like-a-tree-in-the-forest ploy," Stiles said, channeling Don Adams.

"Exactly, except for this one, Guy X. Terminus."

"Who is either an ego case thumbing his nose at everybody, or a doofus who doesn't know any better."

Traci shook her head. "He's for real. A doofus wouldn't know anyone like Crawley."

Stiles opened Dictionary on his PC and typed Terminus into the field. The machine instantly responded.

> Terminus /[L, boundary, end (ca, 1617) 1: a final goal, a finishing point 2: a post or stone marking a boundary 3: the end of a transportation line, also the station, a town or city at such a place: TERMINAL. 4: an extreme point or element: <the *terminus* of a glacier>

"Shit, why didn't he just name himself Terminal in the first place?"

"Maybe he likes Latin," Traci said. "I hated Latin."

"Because he's challenging us." Stiles gave a deep sigh. "If it's a puzzle, it's a tough one. Let's see, what do we know about Terminals?"

"Well, there's Terminal Island."

Stiles perked up. "And X means ex. Somebody who was there."

He used the squad room landline to call Terminal Island Federal Prison. After identifying himself as a detective at the LAPD Hollywood Devision, he was connected to a Supervisor. He asked that the Supervisor e-mail him the T. I. Inmate Release File dating from January first to present.

The list appeared a few minutes later in a PDF file. The two detectives discovered that Guy X. Terminus was their former bank robber arrestee Victor Krait, and that Krait was almost certainly the killer of Clyde Crawley.

Raymondo knew all about explosives. It was a point of pride to be able to discuss these things with his crew of *maleantes*. To be so casual about such tools of violence earned him their respect.

The mere chemical names were chilling—RDX mixed with polysobutylene and di (2-ethylhexyl). All in a little flat cake the size of a pack of cigarettes. A blast of C-4 was so acute it could not be shielded against or outrun. With this kind of power he would blow Jack Stiles and his car into eternity.

Provided with binoculars and Carina's description, Raydo began to shadow Jack Stiles. He learned of Stiles' place of work, his schedule, his personal vehicle, a 2009 Solara coupe. He found that the detective often parked at night near a West Hollywood community park no bigger than two basketball courts end to end. Why Stiles parked there was of no concern. Raydo concentrated on the car. It would be locked, but that was no obstacle. He'd been a skilled car thief at the age of eighteen.

The lights of the park were turned off after eleven o'clock. Two hours later Raydo approached the vehicle, satchel in hand. Within sixty seconds he had slim-jimmed the passenger door. Inside, he used a penlight in his mouth to see.

This wouldn't take long. He slid the driver's seat back a couple of notches and shoved the cake of C-4 under it. Lamp cord was already attached to the cap. He ran the wiring under the floor mat and up the back of the steering column. Using a tool borrowed from his cousin, he pulled the ignition. It was a basic unit with only four terminals. He removed wires from two of them, then twisted one lamp cord lead under the screw of a terminal and tightened it. He twisted the second lead and heard a click.

An enormous explosion hurled the car six feet in the air, fully enveloped in billowing orange flame. A storm of steel, sheet metal, glass and vinyl rained down on a plain of burning asphalt. Wheels rolled down the street like runaway donuts. Most of Raydo's incinerated body lay smoking on the park's blackened turf.

Carina was shocked. "God have mercy, I can't believe he could be so sloppy."

"It's proof of the old saying," Krait sighed. "Never send a boy to do a man's work."

She smiled at that. "There's the bad and the good, querido. Jack Stiles is still alive, still unpunished. But now I have you all to myself. No more Raymondo treating me like a *bruja*."

"You have a most picante way of expressing it."

"Foo, let us celebrate the occasion."

"Of course, my love," he said. "But tomorrow I must buy a car. It's not fair to keep borrowing yours."

"I don't mind."

"I know, and that is sweet. But give me a lift to that CarMart place, and we will both be mobile."

In the morning, it turned out just as he said. Krait found what he was seeking, a four-year-old beige Honda Civic, the most anonymous car on the road. He made the down payment with one of the checks that foolish bank had given him. All well and good, he mused as they drove away. But his thoughts turned to Stiles. No doubt the Hollywood detective would be more vigilant from now on. A new death plan would have to be devised.

As for Stiles himself, he would be driving a pool car for a while. When Nathan heard about the bombing, he was shocked. He issued Jack a key to the condo building's secured parking level. It was the least he could do for his LAPD girl.

9

Evidence gathered from the blast was analyzed by the LAPD
Scientific Investigation Division. The main explosive agent was
identified as RDX because of traces of its polyisobutylene binder.
Known sources of the product would have to confirm that analysis.
From the shredded body, technicians were able to isolate sufficient
DNA to run through the Los Angeles County's new Criminal
Records data base.

A match was made to known felon Raymondo Luna. John
Luttwak ordered his narcotics team to round up Luna's closest
confederates in crime. Under intense questioning, one of them
coughed up Luna's relationship with Carina Parra, the widow
of Raphael Parra. The whole Homicide table knew who Parra
was—the bank robber that Jack Stiles had shot to death. Circles
within circles, Luttwak mused. He was always amazed at the turns
a case could take.

"You're looking rather soignée tonight," Stiles said to Traci.

"I've been called a lot of things, but not soignée."

The two detectives were lounging on Traci's sofa again,
drinking Clos du Bois. She was in the flimsy date dress, the one
she'd worn at The Full Clip. Close to him now, the effect was even
more pleasing.

"Sometimes I wonder," he said.

"About what?"

"Whether I should make an honest woman of you."

"Is that a proposal, detective?"

"If you like. I do love you, in case you haven't been paying attention."

"Whoa, now I've heard everything."

She held her glass aside and gave him a hint-of-apple-and-oak kiss. "If you did propose, I'd say no," she said. "It's so exciting the way it is. But of course it wasn't my car that got blown up down the street."

"I don't care. The Solara had over eighty thousand on the clock."

"What'll you get next?"

"Another coupe, I suppose. We'll drive up to Santa Barbara on our off time. We'll dine out, and listen to jazz, and fuck each other blind."

"And run into somebody from work."

"Yeah, one of McKnight's spies digging clams."

"I love the image," she laughed. "Seriously, let's not change a thing. I know it has its risks, but it's so perfect, so sublime."

"I'll drink to that," he said, drinking to it. "Speaking of the bombing, I don't know how that guy Luna fits in, but I have a feeling that Victor Krait is behind it."

"He'd love to see you dead, that I know."

"And you too. You're the one who poked a Glock up his nose."

"I'll bet Parra's wife and Krait are in this together."

"How prescient of you, detective. Let's bring Carina in for an interview as a person of interest."

"Okay, but no more cop talk." She rose and freed her shoulders from their spaghetti straps. A zip and a wiggle and the little dress slid to the floor.

"Isn't that neat?" she said.

Considering the strong probability that Terminus was Victor Krait, John Luttwak asked himself what must be lurking in that criminal's clever mind. Frustration, of course, from knowing that his orchestration of the death of Jack Stiles had failed. But beyond that were related issues, such as the financing of his plans.

Krait surely had paid Raymondo Luna a fairly large amount in cash for his services. Krait was not the type who buries cash in a satchel somewhere, Luttwak knew. More likely he would've maintained an offshore account that he could access at any time. He could deposit checks here payable to Guy X. Terminus, and then withdraw cash when needed.

Luttwak assigned a staff member to issue an LAPD Criminal Alert to all banks in Los Angeles to check their current depositors for the name Guy X. Terminus. He also issued Krait's bank robbery booking photos to the media. Unfortunately the photos in no way resembled the polished citizen that Krait portrayed today.

Irv Miller and Kaz Kazurian escorted Carina into the interview room, which was a cheerless pale green. She sat at a table that was bolted to the floor. The detectives didn't feel the need to use the table's handcuffs. Miller slid in opposite her. Miller was a heavy man with rimless glasses. In his own low-key way he was able to coax gems of information from unsuspecting subjects. He turned on a recorder and stated the date and the DR number, and who was present. Kazurian stood against the wall, silent and enigmatic.

Carina's file photo didn't do her justice, Miller thought. This dark-haired beauty shared the Zeta-Jones gene set.

"Would you like coffee, Mrs. Parra?" Kazurian asked.

"Yes, that would help." He left and returned with coffee in a paper cup with little fold-out handles.

"I'm Detective Miller," Irv led off. "And this is Detective Kazurian. Please don't be nervous, this is just an interview and you are not under arrest."

"That's a relief. So why am I here?"

"This is in regard to the death of Raymondo Luna. We believe the bombing was an attempt to assassinate an LAPD detective."

"Yes, I saw something about it on the news. But what has that to do with me?"

"We have information that you knew Raymondo Luna."

She sipped the coffee. "Who?"

"Please, Mrs. Parra," Kazurian broke in. "We know from several sources that Luna was your boyfriend."

"All right, I knew him. But he was nothing to me." Miller sensed that at least that part was true.

"And you also knew Detective Stiles, or knew of him, correct?"

"Detective who?"

Kazurian again. "Mrs. Parra, do you believe in God?" Kaz knew that if a question like that were asked in court, counsel would instantly object. But this was not in court.

"Yes, of course."

"Then please stop being evasive and help us get the information we need."

Carina took a deep breath. "I didn't really know him, only his name."

"And you also knew that he was the officer that shot your husband."

"Yes."

"So in the car bombing, you knew both the bomber and the intended victim."

"I knew Raymondo Luna, but only in a superficial way."

"All right," Miller said. "Would you like some more coffee? A cigarette, anything?"

"No, nothing."

To Kazurian he said, "Would you get me a cup, Kaz?" This was code for leave the room. Kazurian left without comment.

"Mrs. Parra, would you mind if I call you Carina? My name is Irv. Perhaps it would make things go a little easier."

"I don't care."

"Good. Let me ask you this, Carina. Can you think of any reason why Ramondo Luna would want to kill detective Stiles?"

"He probably thought it would make points with me. Actually I've come to believe that the detective fired in the line of duty. As for Raymondo, I didn't like him at all."

"Then why didn't you kick him out?"

Her eyes began to mist a little. Miller offered her a tissue.

"Sorry." She dabbed. "I was afraid of him. Raydo was a violent man. His idea of sex was to rape me."

It was time for the strikeout pitch.

"Carina, do you know a man named Victor Krait?"

Miller caught a slight deflection. He knew he had touched a nerve.

"There was a man named Victor Krait years ago. He was a friend of my father's. I have no idea where he is now."

"Did you have a relationship with Victor Krait?"

"I barely knew him."

"Was your relationship with Krait of a sexual nature?"

"Of course not." Another nerve tick.

"Perhaps you would like to reconsider? He is a reasonably handsome man."

"Why do you ask me this? I do not have such feelings for him."

"You mean in your memory, Carina, or now?"

She saw her mistake. "I haven't seen Victor since he . . ."

"Was released from Federal Prison?"

"Stop. I'm not going to answer any more questions without having a lawyer present."

"Oh, that won't be necessary. Remember, you aren't being accused of anything." Miller turned off the tape recorder and opened the door for her.

"Thank you for coming in, Ms. Parra. Here's my card in case you think of anything else. And please be aware that if anything comes up, we may need to talk to you further. I'll have an officer escort you to your car."

10

Luttwak looked out the door of his office. Seeing Stiles at his desk, he motioned him over.

"Have a seat, Jack." He moved some files from his sofa and they sat down.

"What's up, Lieutenant?" Stiles said.

"Something's nagging at me about that blast. What was your car doing a block from Traci's apartment?"

"I was with her discussing Department business."

"Then why didn't you park in front?"

"That's a fair question. I'm a little wary about being seen with her off duty."

"So what were you talking about?"

"Whether Carina Parra and Victor Krait were co-conspirators."

Luttwak was uncomfortable with the way this was going. "Sorry, Jack. It's just that the Captain brought it up."

"You mean Uptight McKnight?"

He had to laugh. "Yeah, him. Get out of here, Jack."

That evening at Musso's, Luttwak talked about his concerns with his Behavioral Psychologist wife Diane.

"You know how much I admire Jack and Traci," he said to her. "They're both talented detectives. But I suspect they're intimately involved. And I don't know what to do about it."

"Why should you do anything about it?" she said.

"Department policy. You know the concept—that partners having an affair can't properly focus on the Job."

"What about us, darling? When you had my skirt up to my frillies at my place did your performance suffer?"

"I hope not."

"And the word 'affair' is so archaic. It sounds like Cary Grant and Grace Kelly sneaking a kiss behind the potted palms."

"So your clinical analysis and recommendation is—"

"Do nothing. Just let them be in love."

Stiles answered his cell phone in the night. It was Ted Redfern, a detective he knew at Rampart. The phone showed the time was 3:15. Instantly he knew something crucial was happening.

"What's up, Ted," he said.

"Turn on your TV to channels 2, 4, 7, or 9. They've got that fucker Topo holed up in his house with three or four other pukes. He's wanted in our jurisdiction for robbery, grand theft auto and gang activity. Did I mention arms trafficking?"

"And you think he's good for bombing my car."

"Exactly."

"Thanks, buddy. I'll buy you a drink at The Clip."

"I hoped you'd say that."

Channel 9 had the best coverage, this being the stuff they thrived on. Their helicopter was circling high above, recording the scene through a 500mm Canon lens. Below, a police chopper was using a "night sun" floodlight to illuminate the suspects' house and yard. Several patrol cars were positioned front and back with their light bars flashing. Officers were busy evacuating residents from nearby houses. Lieutenant Walter Price, Luttwak's opposite number at Rampart, was in charge.

The channel 9 copter pilot was reporting to anchor Susan Sanchez.

"We haven't received an official briefing from the LAPD, but sources familiar with the situation indicate that five known gang members are inside the house. One is reported to be the notorious illegal arms dealer Federico Cruz, known on the streets as Topo."

"I assume he's very dangerous, Kevin," Sanchez said.

"Undoubtedly. He's an illegal with a long sheet, as they say, and four years' time served. Incredibly, he's never been turned over to U. S. Immigration and Customs Enforcement—commonly known as ICE."

"Is that because of Special Order 40?"

"Not really, Susan. Special Order 40 was issued by the LAPD in 1979. It says you can't ask people about their immigration status for no reason. Only when suspects are actually under arrest, can ICE be informed."

Stiles was no fan of Special Order 40. More than once he'd arrested an illegal on a felony charge, and later found him on the streets—and arrested him all over again.

The chopper pilot again. "Susan, SWAT team members are starting to arrive in their own cars. The SWAT commander is taking over the scene from Lieutenant Price. That's normal procedure in SWAT call-ups."

"Not like in TV crime shows."

"Not even close. Now we can see the SWAT officers getting helmets and armor and assault weapons out of their car trunks. The SWAT Commander has relieved the LAPD and they are pulling back from their positions."

Coffee from his plug-in coffee maker had gone tepid as Stiles continued to watch. In a brief glimpse, the police chopper crossed below the Channel 9 craft. Half an hour went by, while nothing new was happening. The TV anchor and the Channel 9 pilot were repeating everything they knew, simply expressing it in different words.

It was time for Stiles to head for work. Just as he was strapping on his belt, the SWAT commander ordered a barrage of tear gas. Stiles watched while gray smoke issued from the house's smashed windows. Heavily armed and masked troops stormed the house and dragged five eye-stung, choking gangsters out onto the lawn and cuffed them. Federico Cruz was among the five.

Victor Krait watched the crime opera on the flat screen TV at Carina's house. He was unaware that the detectives had discovered who Guy X. Terminus was. But Carina, as Parra's widow, would be questioned about the bombing, and perhaps surveilled. He no longer could risk staying with her. Still, he desired the beautiful and sexy Latina. He would find a way to continue seeing her.

To boost his available resources, another visit to the bank was in order. There he filled out a withdrawal slip for another few thousand. A different teller served him this time. When she walked toward the vault, Krait noticed that she stopped to make a phone call. Instantly he sensed that she was calling the police. He made an excuse and left the building.

From a store across the street he watched a two-man patrol car arrive. So, they did know about him. The Terminus identity that he'd killed for was now useless.

This was disappointing but far from fatal. Krait knew exactly what he needed to do. He would revert to his former modus operandi, just as his father had taught him—"Don't get cute, Victor. Do what you know." He hated the way the old man kept treating him like a fool. Still, he'd inherited his father's genes. He would follow the instincts that had served him well.

Federico Cruz was remanded by Judge Thelma Pinchaud on arms trafficking charges. The array of assault rifles, handguns, boxes of ammunition and explosives found at his premises was good enough for her. She rejected counsel's request to deny the police the right to question him about other crimes. Detective Stiles could not participate, however, because of his status as a putative victim.

Dick Cheevers and Ed Chase conducted Cruz to the interview room. Chase, the thin lipped hard-nosed give-no-quarter cop, would start the questioning. He took a moment to stare at Cruz's bandido mustache and stained teeth grinning at him. Cheevers stood by the door.

"Ah, Topo," Chase said. "I see you finally stepped on your weenie."

"Fuck you, cop." Topo rattled the cuffs that lashed him to the table.

Chase laughed. "Is that the best you can do?"

"Where's my lawyer, dog pile?" This was Max Tischler, counsel to the gangs, defender of killers and rapists.

"He's on his way. He's stuck in traffic right now."

"So gimme a cigarette, and we wait."

"Sorry, there's no smoking in the building."

"The whole building will get smoked as soon as I get out of here."

Chase ignored this wisecrack. "Do you know somebody named Raymondo Luna?"

"No."

"Let me refresh your memory. He's the moron you sold the C-4 to."

Topo laughed. "What is C-4, your cock size?"

"C-4 is what we found kilos of at your pad, along with enough assault rifles, 9mm handguns, and ammo to start a war."

"I don' seen no fuckin' weapons."

"Your prints were all over them. Your clothes reeked with RDX."

"Fuckin' LAPD planted those."

At this point Cheevers said, "Don't waste any more time on this putz. He's going away for twenty to life."

"My lawyer will get me a deal, like always."

Chase smiled. "No way. Clarence Darrow couldn't get you off."

"Who's he?"

At that moment Tischler actually did arrive. He was short, fat and smarmy. His suit was Italian made, and his polaroids were by Calvin Klein.

"How nice to see you detectives again," he greeted.

"You too, attorney," Cheevers said. "Mr. Cruz been asking for you. He's a pretty hard case."

"Fuckers are abusing me," Topo croaked.

"Don't worry, we'll talk and we'll see what can be worked out for you."

"There's just a teeny problem with that," Chase said. "No way is the Federal ADA going to play your little games."

11

At summer daybreak, Victor Krait walked down an alley in back of some expensive homes along Franklin Avenue. He wore a white jumpsuit he bought at a uniforms outlet. He carried a clip board full of official-looking forms. If anyone questioned him he would identify himself as an inspector from the Sanitation Department. If all else failed he still carried his pistol.

It wasn't long before he had found what he was looking for, a trash bin containing discarded financial mail to someone named Calvin A. Scott. Some were bank statements showing check images and account numbers. Others were month-end credit card bills and a notice from Medicare carrying his Social Security number. Also a cold pitch from Visa offering a pre-approved platinum card.

Perfect. He would transfer his First Hollywood deposits to Scott's bank. Krait would now become Calvin A. Scott, Bank of America account holder.

John Luttwak had spent most of the morning with his Auto Theft units. Now, at 1015 hours, he summoned the Homicide team that inherited the Crawley case to the conference room. Detectives Irv Miller and Kaz Kazurian pulled up chairs and sat down with their laptops, note pads, pens, coffee mugs and power drinks. Luttwak's mood was one of frustration.

"We've got a pair of related crimes on our hands," Luttwak began. "The Crawley shooting, a homicide, and the bombing of Jack's car, an attempted homicide. I know you've submitted your Investigative Reports, but let's review. At this point what do we actually know?"

Miller opened the file in his laptop. "We know that Crawley was killed by Victor Krait, aka Guy X. Terminus, to try to cover his false identity tracks."

"Can we prove that?"

"I think so. We have means, motive, opportunity, and FBI ballistics and trace evidence. All that's missing is Krait."

"We know he was living with Carina Parra," Kazurian said. "Knowing Krait, he is screwing her. They knew each other before Krait was sent to T.I. It's possible they both want to kill Jack Stiles, but for different reasons."

"And Traci Little. She's the one who arrested Krait."

"Could be," Miller said. "But Jack is the man who went after Parra and the money bag. He ran down Parra and killed him. That makes him target one."

"It's a damn good thing Raymondo blew himself up," Luttwak said, "or this would be a different meeting."

Miller again. "We also know Raymondo was still with Carina at the time. She has to know what went down."

"Trust me," Kazurian said. "That little hottie is in it up to her ass."

"Our bank alert for Guy X. Terminus got a hit," Miller said. "First Hollywood's Security tapes confirm that it really is Krait. He deposited multi-thousands of dollars from a Swiss account into the bank, then made large cash withdrawals to work with. The bank's tapes also show Krait getting out of Carina's car. We could call in the Secret Service if we wanted to."

"I hate that," Luttwak said. "The Feds always throw their weight around."

"Borrowing her car would crimp Krait's style, so he's probably got himself other wheels by now."

"Okay, follow up on that," Luttwak said. "What else?"

"Krait has probably changed identities again. We almost nailed him at First Hollywood, but somehow he saw it coming. The man is very clever, very resourceful."

Luttwak summed it up. "Great, so we've got a suspect genius who has no name, no location, and lots of cash."

"Hey, how easy can things get?" Kaz said.

"When are they ever?" Luttwak said. "I'm assigning some SIS units to surveil Carina at her home." SIS was Special Investigation Section. "They'll follow her car and see where she goes, what she does. Meanwhile you two are up next. I want you to cover that celebrity murder that happened in the wee hours this morning."

Miller and Kazurian drove up Laurel Canyon and turned left at Lookout Mountain. This was the playground of David Carradine, Burt Reynolds, Tennessee Williams and other fabled figures. Farther on, Wonderland Avenue led them into a maze of narrow uphill roads. Using their satellite system, they followed a dead end road leading to the gated chateau of soap opera queen Alyissa Durant.

Three black and whites and a Field Unit van were parked near the open gate. Yellow tape stapled to various nearby trees defined the crime scene. Nearby, a Channel 7 news team was already reporting.

The detectives showed their ID badge wallets to a patrolman and walked up a brick entrance way to the front door. Inside, they could see an LAPD team photographing the scene and logging various scrapings and swabbings.

They spoke to sergeant David Keyes.

"What have we got, sergeant?" Miller said.

"A homicide by blunt force," Keyes said. "A really messy one. The victim must have put up a fight, judging from the blood all over the place."

"Weapon?"

"A bronze Statue of Liberty, the kind people collect from gift shops."

"Ah, the proverbial weapon of opportunity."

"Her body lies right where it fell, no drag marks or anything."

"Okay let's have a look."

It was a gruesome scene, shocking even to experienced officers. Alyissa Durant was lying in front of the fireplace in a lake crimson, her head and features beaten beyond recognition. Blood was sprayed everywhere, on her gown, on the bricks, on the walls and the nearby furniture. The bloody statue rested at her feet.

Medical examiner Norm Nomura himself was present for this one.

"What a frugly mess this is, Norm," Kazurian said to him. "One of the worst I've ever seen."

"Yeah, for me too. I always hate to see someone this feisty go down."

"Does she have family here, do you know?"

"A couple of nieces back east. She was formerly married to Morse Brenner, a producer you may recall. He ended up on our slab with an overdose a few years back. Now there's a boyfriend, I hear. You guys will probably want to interview him."

"Yep," Kaz said, terse as ever.

The boyfriend turned out to be aspiring actor Tony Fortuna. Two days later they found him at a Hollywood hot pillow motel in the company of a fake blonde named Nikki Raye. Tony and Nikki were interviewed separately at Hollywood Division as persons of interest in the Durant murder.

Fortuna wasn't happy.

"You've got no right to bring me in here. I don't know anything about Alyssa getting killed." He got up to leave, and Miller had to sit him down again.

"Relax, Tony," Miller said. "We're just going to talk. If you want a lawyer, we'll bring one in for you."

"What do I need with a lawyer? I didn't do anything."

"Okay. All we want is your cooperation." He turned on the tape machine.

"You're pretty strong, Tony. Anybody ever tell you that?"

"I work out. Look, I didn't do any killing. I was with Nikki when it happened."

"How do you know when that was?"

Fortuna sneered, "We saw it on the news."

"The news didn't say when it happened, just when her body was discovered. But maybe you know when it happened because you were there."

"No way, off-i-cer."

"So if you're innocent, you won't mind if we take a DNA sample, right?"

Fortuna began to pay attention. "Hey, I'm totally innocent here. I loved Alyssa and I wouldn't do a thing to hurt her."

"No? What about cheating on her with Nikki Raye? You were in bed with Nikki when last seen."

"Nikki is just recreation, just another wet pussy out there in HollyPussyWood."

"By the way, what happened to your finger?" This referred to his right index finger, which had a BandAid on it.

"I caught it in my fly."

Kazurian said, "Okay, we're about done. A quick cheek swab and you're out of here." Anxious to leave, Fortuna complied.

Nikki Raye's reaction to Hollywood station was one of awe. She was spacey enough to begin with, but when she walked into the busy squad room, her eyes got as big as saucers.

"Is this where they made that L.A. Confidential?"

"Close enough," Kazurian said.

They sat at the table in the cheerless interview room. It was another shock when she saw the handcuffs dangling from the table.

"Are you gonna use those on me?"

"No. You're not under arrest. You're here as a person of interest. We'd like your help."

Miller got right to it, before any more skidding. "This is regarding the murder of Alyssa Durant."

"Oh, I saw that on the news. Poor Alyssa."

"Tell us about her."

"Well, she is really sweet. She treated me like a daughter. My boyfriend Tony worked for her."

"That would be Tony Fortuna?" Kaz said.

"Yeah, he's so cool. He drives a Jagwire XJ. It's midnight blue."

Let her run on, Miller decided. "Well, here's the thing. Tony is one of our suspects in the murder."

"Oh, Tony wouldn't do anything like that. Tony and Alyssa were tight. He handled her business contracts, and like that. She was always giving him stuff, like cufflinks or a cigarette case."

"Were they having an affair, do you know?"

"No, I take care of Tony. See, I go down and take his cock and—"

"Actually, you are Tony's alibi. He has testified that the two of you were together at the time of the murder."

Nikki was too anxious to confide. "We were having sex at the Sunset Tropics. That's not illegal, is it?"

"No, but you might want to change your mind about super-cool Tony."

Miller inserted a tape into the machine. "This is a recording of Tony's interview yesterday."

Nikki listened with an open mouth as the tape rolled. Her normally googley eyes turned to slits when she heard Fortuna spout his true opinion of her.

"Is this tape real?"

"As real as it gets. Tony wasn't with you that night, was he."

"No."

"We didn't think so," Kaz said. "What you just said, along with his bitten finger will nail him for this. The question now is whether you're going down with him. We can't help you unless you tell us the full and faithful truth."

"That fuckwad! I told him not to do it, but he wouldn't listen."

12

Krait's first move as Calvin A. Scott was to send in the Visa card application along with a change of address to his newly rented quarters. Next, he visited the DMV and reported that he'd lost his wallet, including his driver's license. He filled out the paperwork, signing with a reasonable version of Scott's signature. After visiting two more windows, he stood for photograph, paid a fee, and was issued a temporary license.

Ten days went by. Krait received license Z570572 from Sacramento with the usual hazy mug shot and Scott's forged signature. Two days later a platinum Visa card arrived. The gushy covering letter informed him that his credit limit would be $15, 000.

It was all so easy. Victor Krait would now become Calvin A. Scott, wealthy new player.

At Hollywood station's detective squad room, Traci e-mailed the Los Angeles County Automobile Dealer's Association requesting a search of their records for the name Guy X. Terminus, a felon wanted for murder. LAPD heads-ups of this sort were generally treated seriously. By late afternoon Stiles and Traci were fairly sure that Krait hadn't purchased a new car. Phone calls to the major used car dealers, however, yielded a hit. Guy X. Terminus had purchased a Honda Civic from CarMart at their South Sepulveda Boulevard lot.

Stiles would handle this one himself. He checked out an unmarked sedan from the pool and drove to the CarMart lot. The manager was Howard Resnik, a pudgy man with a black dyed comb-over.

"What can CarMart do to assist you, detective?" Resnik said.

"I need for you to check your files as to a car purchase by Guy X. Terminus."

Resnik turned to his computer. "Our alpha list for this month and last will have it." Two mouse clicks and it was on the screen. "Here it is. Terminus, June 26th."

Stiles looked over Resnik's shoulder to read the entry.

Honda Civic LX, VIN 39307822. License tag is 5NUV3884. Color, Champagne.

Sale price: $13, 988, with 36 months financing.

Purchaser: Guy X. Terminus

Address: P. O. Box 314, SpeedPrint store
12072 Pico Boulevard, Los Angeles, CA 90033
Telephone: 323-654-7511

"I remember the man," Resnik said. He looked a little like Jeremy Irons, the actor. Ordinarily we don't trust somebody with only a box number, but it was late in the month and the guy was there, cash in hand."

"Can you print that transaction for me?" Stiles said.

"No problemo." Resnik printed it and handed it to him.

"Thanks. On another subject, do you by chance have a late model Lexus coupe? Maybe silver?"

"Probably do. Let me check."

"I don't have time right now, but I'll be in touch."

Resnik got up and shook his hand. "Remember, for the LAPD we always give a price break."

On Pico, Stiles stopped at the SpeedPrint store. There was no such box number.

Stiles entered the I-10 on-ramp and headed east toward Hollywood. It had been a useful trip, he mused. That license tag number would be very useful in tracking down Krait. And that car deal might work out too.

Just west of La Brea, Stiles noticed a CHP cruiser that had stopped a dark blue Ford sedan. The officer was standing by his driver's door with his hand on his gun, calling in his location. Inside the Ford, Stiles could see three tattooed gang members moving around, getting their pistols ready.

Stiles slowed and pulled over behind the Highway Patrol car. He radioed his position, unlocked his shotgun and got out of his car. He showed his badge, and called out, "LAPD Hollywood. I'll back you up!" The CHP officer acknowledged. He approached on the left, Stiles on the right. When Stiles closed to fifteen feet, he jacked a round into the shotgun's chamber. When the gangsters heard that sound, any thoughts of resistance evaporated.

Following the CHP's commands, they stepped out with hands on their heads facing away from the two cops. One by one they walked backwards toward them and were cuffed. Stiles stood by while the State officer radioed his RTO, four suspects in custody, request assistance. Within minutes a Highway Patrol van arrived at the scene. The arresting CHP officer thanked Stiles and they shared a high five.

Stiles drove away with a sense of satisfaction. He strongly believed in inter-agency support, a fundamental concept in law enforcement. At the Full Clip that night, the incident became one of a handful of stories told at the bar.

Victor Krait, acting as Calvin A. Scott, began a series of moves that marked his strategy. It began with withdrawals at Bank of America branches far from the one where Scott himself was known. Over two week's time, he drained Scott's money market account of most of its funds, a ready cash infusion of several thousand dollars. Concurrently, he used Scott's Visa card to borrow up to three quarters of its credit limit. Not until Scott's July statements arrived would he realize his identity had been stolen. By then it would be too late.

This was a familiar game to Victor Krait. These and similar scams had filled his Zurich numbered account well before the failed bank robbery that put him in Terminal Island. It was his move now. He knew exactly what he wanted. As Calvin Scott, he would create a new life with no relationship whatever to Carina Parra.

Dick Cheevers and Ed Chase were checking for late night action at Carina's house. They were holed up in an Ugly Duckling car across the street and two doors down. The LAPD rented most of their undercover cars from Ugly Duckling because of their anonymity. Carina's car was parked in the driveway, so it was likely she was at home. In the front windows of the house the blinds were drawn. All they could see was the faint reflecting light from a television set. The two detectives talked, if only not to fall asleep.

Cheevers was married, Chase was not.

"How you doing with that girl from the Valley, man?" Cheevers asked him.

"Jennifer? It was terrific while it lasted, but we broke up," Chase said.

"Whoa, what happened?"

"At first she was excited to be dating a cop. I mean the sex was really great. Then one night at her place, my cell rang and I got called in. She discovered that the LAPD always comes first."

"Tell me about it," Cheevers said. "Xynthia's not a truly happy camper with cop work either, all the shit that goes with it. She hates when I been to the range. She makes me wash up first thing even though there's no odor."

"She's probably worried about you getting shot on duty."

"That too."

"Of course some women are okay with police work," Chase said. "Reminds me of that Academy probationer Arianna, who did her work in the bull pen. A really hot lookin' girl too—her supervisor's fingerprints were all over her. Finally she filed a sexual harassment suit."

"I do remember Arianna," Cheevers said. "Somebody must have been protecting the Supe, because she got transferred out to North Hollywood."

"No doubt. Anyway, she continued in the office at North Hollywood and became a Sergeant. Then a lieutenant, and then a Captain. She's a supervisor herself now, I heard. And all that with no street experience!"

"Wonders never cease, man."

Chase broke out some power bars. "They have these in the slot machines now. It's actually good for you, keeps your pecker up."

At 0200 hours they shut down for the night.

13

Carina received a message by a simple device. A ten-year-old boy knocked on her front door and handed the envelope to her. The message read,

> *Drive to the Westside Shopping Mall at 4 pm.*
> *Park in the north Macy's lot and enter the store.*
> *Buy anything you want and exit the south side.*
> *Get into the blue minivan with the smoked*
> *windows.*
>
> *V.*

Carina smiled at the delivery mode. It was so mysterious, so romantic.

Day watch, an SIS unit reported Carina's car pulling out of her driveway. Miller and Kazurian took over. They followed Carina as she drove west on Santa Monica past Beverly Hills. This was the first trip Carina had made in the five days of observation.

It wasn't a new thrill in aesthetics. The old car tracks down the middle of the divided street were torn up in preparation for a light rail project. The streets both ways looked grubby, lined with thirty-year-old aluminum storefronts and fast food places all the way to the Westside Mall.

Carina entered the Macy's store and took the escalator to the lingerie department. Miller and Kaz followed, observing from a distance. They watched Carina consider various flimsy items and finally choose one. They had no way of knowing it was a baby doll just like the one Raymondo had ripped off her. She used a charge card and left the department carrying a white bag with the red Macy's logo.

On the first level again, Carina toured the central cosmetics and jewelry aisle, pausing only to be sprayed with scent by a thin woman in a black dress and pearls. The detectives followed, trying not to look like shoplifters. Finally she exited to the south lot and stepped into a blue van and was driven away.

"Shit, we lost her," Kazurian said.

"Dig the plate holder. It's a Hertz rental."

Kaz was writing. "I've got the number, but it'll be under some phony name."

"We still have Carina's car at the North end," Miller said.

"She'll just say she went for a drink with her girlfriend from Deer Whistle, Kansas."

"I suppose so."

"I'd love to see that hottie in whatever she bought."

"Yeah, me too."

Half an hour later Carina was at the Holiday Inn straddling Victor Krait, with the new baby doll draped over the bedpost.

Dick Cheevers got home at 2:30 AM. The house, a Hollywood cottage built in the Nathanael West era, stood silently in the dim cast of its porch light and a streetlight two doors down, hardly the lively place it normally was on a sunny day in summer. After parking in the driveway, he entered through the front door. He unhooked his belt and stowed it with his Beretta on the top shelf of his bookcase. In the fridge he found half a carton of apple juice and chugged it down in one tilt.

In the bedroom he found Xynthia only half awake. "What time is it, hon?" she asked.

"Two thirty." He undressed and slid in beside her.

"Is everything okay out there?"

"Yeah, but I'm bone weary, all this night duty."

"Excuses, excuses. You just want to catch a look at that hot Latina girl."

He wrapped his big arms around her. "Not hot as you, babe. And anyway, we're getting overtime."

"Mm, that I like."

"Actually, it's boring as hell. You sit there like a lump of coal and nothing happens. And then, more nothing happens. You drink coffee, eat junk food out of a bag, look at your watch. Fifteen minutes have gone by. You talk trivia with your partner. Your eyelids get droopy and you doze off. Your partner kicks your butt. By the time your watch ends, your eyes are glazed over."

"Poor baby."

"So how'd Jamal do today?" This was Cheevers' tenth-grader.

"He did good, but now he wants a tattoo."

"Man, the kids grow up in a hurry these days, don't they."

"All the kids have tattoos, he says."

"We can't blame him, really. The dudes all know his daddy is a cop. Jamal is okay with that, but he wants to look more like them. I'll talk to him."

"Okay, but please, not a skull on fire, or a dagger with blood dripping."

"Right. Maybe he can have a mermaid. They can ink it so when he flexes his biceps she wiggles her tail. That oughta get him some street cred."

"Honestly, you two are a pair." She gave him a kiss. "Mm, you got into that apple juice, didn't you."

Luttwak's detectives were unaware of Krait's newest identity, but now they had his car to work with. It wasn't much, but least it was something. They issued an All-Points Bulletin for suspect Victor Krait aka Guy X. Terminus, driving a Honda Civic LX sedan, tag number 5NUV3884. Suspect is armed and dangerous. Do not approach without back-up.

That same day, the real Calvin Scott reported his losses to the LAPD's city-wide Bunko Forgery Division. Seriously overworked, they dished it off to Hollywood. At the time, no one had a clue that the Calvin Scott matter was related in any way to Victor Krait.

Surveillance of Carina's car, still parked at Macy's, continued. Two days later at 2130 hours, Carina hurried across the mostly empty parking lot from the direction of the freeway service road. Irv and Kaz were immediately dispatched to pick her up.

Carina was upset. "You two again? Why are you harassing me like this?"

"We need to talk," Miller said.

"I've already told you all that I know."

"Some new issues have come up," Kaz said.

"What new issues?"

"That's what we're going to talk about."

"I need a day to arrange for a lawyer."

"No problem." Kaz gave her a business card. "You can reach us at this number."

The following afternoon, Carina appeared at Hollywood station, accompanied by scented and manicured Marvin Feasel, esq. Miller and Kazurian had never met Feasel before, yet he looked familiar. We must have seen his mug in the yellow pages, Miller figured. Also present was Federal ADA James Presley. After introductions, the group sat down at the table. Coffee was provided in foam cups. Miller switched on a recorder and stated the date, persons present, case number, and other such precursors.

"Mrs. Parra is here to testify fully and truthfully in aid of your investigation," Feasel said.

"Understood," Miller said. "Ms. Parra, you are here as a person of interest, not as a murder suspect. At this point, we'd just like you to tell us what you know."

"At this point? What point is that?"

"First, let's be informal. I'll address you as Carina. You already know me as Irv, and detective Kazurian is known around here as Kaz. Also joining us today will be Assistant District Attorney Jim Presley."

Carina sighed. "I don't care. Just get it over with."

"All right," Miller said, getting right on it. "We want to know why you parked your car at Macy's, went through the store and exited into a rented blue van and drove away."

"How did you know that?"

"You were seen by two detectives working a case at that location."

"I don't understand. I met a friend of mine for lunch. Is that a crime?"

"No, but a two-day lunch is a pretty long one."

"All right, so we did some things together."

"We caught the plate number of the rented vehicle," Miller said. "Do you know anyone name Calvin Scott?" He noted a faint but visible flinch.

"No. Who is he?"

"Perhaps you know him as Victor Krait?"

"I said before, I haven't seen Victor in ages."

"What would you say if we told you we have a security camera tape of Victor driving your car?"

Silence.

"Maybe now would be a good time to stop lying."

Feasel intervened. "Careful, detective. You're browbeating my client." He and Carina huddled over the security tape issue.

"Mrs. Parra will answer the question, but clean up your act, or this interview is over."

Kazurian spoke up, his eyes masked by dark glasses.

"Let's get down to basics, Carina. This investigation is about the premeditated murder of Clyde Crawley and the attempted murder of police detective Jack Stiles. It couldn't be more serious."

"How does that—"

"We believe that Victor Krait is responsible for the bombing of detective Stiles' car. From forensic analysis of the crime scene, we know that the ignition was wired to trigger that bomb, ensuring that detective Stiles would be killed."

"I don't know anything about—"

"We further believe you and Raymondo Luna conspired with Victor Krait in this criminal act."

Carina's head began to turn slowly side to side.

"Do you have any idea what you are into, Ms. Parra?" ADA Presley said. "If you are found guilty of accessory to murder, you could go away for 20 years. No more designer dresses, no more 3-inch heels. No more life style."

"Save yourself, Carina," Miller said. "Don't go down with that vicious killer."

Tears began to trickle down her cheeks.

"Oh God, what can I do?"

At this moment, Feasel intervened. "Give us a moment, detectives. Perhaps we can come to an agreement."

It took only five minutes. "Mrs. Parra will make a complete and comprehensive statement," Feasel offered. "In exchange she will not be charged."

It was Presley's game now. "Will the statement implicate Victor Krait in murder?"

Feasel: "Yes."

"In that case, maybe we can work something out. She'll have to testify, of course."

"Understood."

Kazurian slid a lined yellow pad and a pen over to Carina. "Start writing, and don't leave anything out."

She looked at the pen as if it were a snake. "If Victor finds out about this, he will kill me," she said.

14

Car 8T76, assigned to Traffic, was driven by Hollywood officer Charlie Telford. The night seemed quiet enough and he looked forward to going off watch at midnight. At 2145 hours on a residential street in West Hollywood, Telford spotted a Honda Civic LX running an octagonal stop sign. He turned on his light bar and pulled the car over. Thinking he had a routine traffic stop, he radioed location, make, model and license tag to the RTO. With nothing further, he walked toward the car, his right hand on his service weapon.

Inside the car, Victor Krait waited. He assumed his cover had been broken and he would be arrested. But no way on God's green earth was Krait going back to Terminal Island. He rolled down his window and watched Telford approaching in his side mirror. When the officer was even with the window, Krait fired three rounds into his chest, killing him instantly. He started the Honda and drove away, with the smell of death and smoke still in the air.

Along with dozens of others Stiles attended the funeral, a gloomy occasion complete with bagpipers from the LAPD Emerald Society. It was a cloudy day for July, adding to the general mood of sorrow. The Chaplain addressed the mourners with a message of faith and comfort, and encouraged a few of Charlie's friends to speak of his days among them. He closed with a masterly recitation of the 23rd Psalm.

"The Lord is my shepherd, I shall not want;
He makes me lie down in green pastures.
He leads me beside still waters;
He restores my soul.
He leads me in paths of righteousness
for His name's sake.
Even though I walk through the valley
of the shadow of death, I fear no evil . . ."

Telford was an experienced cop within a few years of retirement. Stiles knew him, in fact most of the detectives did. Stiles knew his wife too. It was going to be hard on Stella and on their son and daughter, both of whom were in law enforcement but in other jurisdictions.

After the service Stiles drove to Stella Telford's Studio City home. As approached he could see the familiar signs of middle class life—a wide one-story Mediterranean style house, a brief but well-kept lawn with a red brick walk, azaleas fronting the entrance, a basketball hoop over the garage door. Two dead newspapers lay in the driveway. The 3-inch white wood shutters in the windows were closed and silence prevailed.

Stiles stood in the brick entranceway and rapped with the brass knocker. Through the blinds Stella recognized a typical detectives pool car. In the door's peep hole, she saw a macro-sized image of Stiles. She opened the door.

"Charlie's gone," she said, that simple.

"I know it," Stiles said, pulling her to him and offering her his shoulder. He could feel her trembling, fighting off tears.

"I worried about him, Jack," Stella said. "Every time he buckled on his gear, he'd say, Don't worry, hon. The guys are out there for me."

"Charlie wasn't the sort of man who'd back down, Stella. And you wouldn't want him to be, either."

"You're right of course, but it hurts. Most of all, Kevin. He's Laura's kid, you know. He always wanted to go to the firing range with Charlie, but Charlie would say, 'Not now, maybe in a couple more years.' But now there's no more years."

He released her and she wiped away the tears with a tissue. "I just have to suck it up, Jack. At least the family is with me. They're coming tonight, bringing all sorts of comfort food, God bless 'em." She took a deep breath. "Can I get you a cold one?"

"Sure, that would be nice." He sat on the brown-striped sofa watching her walk to the kitchen. She was decently dressed but the clothing seemed to belong on a woman ten years younger. Nothing is quite right with anything when a cop dies.

Stella returned with the beer and sat with him.

"How is the job treating you, Jack?"

"As well as could be expected. My partner Traci Little and I are working another case that involves both a murder and an attempted murder."

"It's crazy, Jack. Some people are just determined to kill each other."

"Some people are born to be bad, Stella. They start out kicking the dog, then it's drugs and burglary and auto theft, and finally somebody gets shot."

"Do you ever feel sorry for them?"

"I feel sorry for people living in the ghetto, but that's no license to kill. In fact, most of the time they're the victims. For the sick puppies we're talking about, it's in their blood and no amount of social rescue is going to change them."

Stella sighed. "It's been a long ride. I remember once when Charlie and his partner were working out of Rampart, they were the first car to field a robbery in progress at a 7-eleven. An 18th Street gang member had already shot the counter man and a few customers were still in the store." She looked away as if the scene was playing out in her mind. "Charlie and his partner burst into the store and braced the gangster. The man refused to drop his gun. Instead, he ducked behind counters and displays and fired three or four shots. Charlie got hit in his left thumb. Charlie fired back and killed the suspect dead as a doorknob. I was almost glad about Charlie's thumb. I thought, if that's all that happens to him I can live with it."

"Every cop's wife feels the same way. It's all part of police work."

"I know."

Stiles finished half of the can. "I have to get back on duty, Stella. Next time I'll bring my partner Traci. You remember her?"

"Of course. I'd love to see her."

Stiles hated to leave her in the echoing silence. At the door he took her hands and said, "There's one thing I can tell you, Stella. When Charlie pulled that car over for running a stop sign, he radioed the plate number. We're pretty sure who the shooter was. If we can confirm it we'll track that sick son of a bitch down, and that's a promise. I just hope he resists."

Stiles gave Stella a hug and a kiss, and walked away.

Victor Krait realized that his car could now put him in mortal danger. Every cop in town would be on the lookout for his license plate. Resourceful as ever, he had a ready answer. He bought a copy of Auto Trader at a local supermarket. Paging through it he found a twelve-year-old Chevrolet sedan for sale cheap. The owner's name was Hispanic, possibly a street worker who needed fast money. This was perfect.

Most of Krait's surmise was correct. Salvador Chavez was a part time gardener. He jumped at Krait's offer of cash. Especially, he was thankful that Señor Terminus would handle the registration filing. The deal was struck in a matter of minutes. Krait then dropped off Chavez in his east L.A. neighborhood.

Krait's response to registration filing was to ignore it. What he wanted was Chavez's license plates. He threw out the 5NUV3884 tags of his own car and substituted the Chevy's 4STL2827. He dumped the Chevy off Mulholland Drive into a canyon of dead cars, walked down to Ventura Boulevard and took a bus back to West Hollywood. The only remaining thing to do was to check the DMV for unpaid tickets or fees. Then, as Calvin Scott, he would return to the impending death of Jack Stiles.

The insurance check arrived in the mail. Total loss of one 2009 Toyota Solara coupe, Blue Book value: $11, 699. Comb-over man Howard Resnik had mentioned a discount for LAPD officers. Stiles called him to see what kind of a deal he could work out.

"Thank you for calling CarMart," a soothing female voice answered.

"Howard Resnik please."

When Reznik picked up, Stiles said, "This is detective Jack Stiles, LAPD. We talked a while back, if you recall."

"Yes, detective. Did our search help with that case you were working?"

"It did, but I'm not permitted to talk about it. Actually, my call is in regard to buying a late model Lexus GX. You mentioned a courtesy discount."

"We do offer a five percent law enforcement discount. Let me check our stock."

In three minutes Resnik was back. We do have a 2009 Lexus GX for $33, 888, less the discount. We also have a 2009 Honda CRV for $24, 998 less the discount. Both have under 45K on the clock."

"Thanks, I'll get back to you on that."

The CRV was affordable, Stiles thought. But do I really want a bigger car with fewer horses? Not really. I'm in the mood for something that moves. He called Resnik back.

"Would you happen to have a late model Mustang coupe with a stick shift?"

"Hang on detective." A few minutes ticked away. "No, but we have a 2009 Mustang GT convertible, with manual tranny, 35K on the clock, for $24,988 less the discount. Ten thousand mile warranty. Color red. Is that too flashy for you?"

"No, not at all. What about financing?"

"The usual. Five thousand down and 30 months."

"I can hack that."

A red Mustang convertible. Stiles knew he had to have that car.

15

Firearms analysis received from NIBIN revealed that the gun used to kill Charlie Telford was the same one used in the Crawley murder. This made Victor Krait a double murderer, ever more reckless in the pursuit of his criminal agenda.

In the detectives squad room Traci found Stiles talking on the squad room land line. Who's calling? she wrote on a pad. He wrote Artie. Arthur Friedman, she knew, worked on LAPD's Bunco/Forgery Division.

"No starlets over here," she heard Stiles say. "The only hot girl around here is my partner Traci." She gave him a stiff poke.

Stiles went on. "Hey man, can you give us some help with ID theft? We need a list of ID victims in Hollywood area starting the first of this month."

A short pause. "That would be terrific, Artie. Thanks muchísimo. "I'll let you know if anything works out." Ten minutes later, Stiles' printer blinked green and whirred. Out came a single page of names, addresses and phone numbers.

"This shouldn't take too long," Traci said. She divided the list into two groups of eighteen, and they began calling people to learn how much they had lost.

Most said their ATM had been accessed for cash, and/or their credit cards used to purchase electronics, apparel, and over the counter drugs—the usual small time gang stuff. Only one man reported having his bank accounts drained. He agreed to meet with the detectives.

The house was located one block north of Los Feliz near Griffith Park. It was a Spanish makeover with red tile roofing and a courtyard. Bougainvillea crawled over the trellis as in a watercolor painting. Calvin A. Scott answered the 3-tone door bell. He was a tall man in his sixties with white hair and a spotted scalp.

"We're the officers who called you, Mr. Scott," Stiles said. "I'm Detective Stiles and this is Detective Little. They showed him their IDs and badges.

"Come in, officers," Scott said, and showed them into his living room. August daylight swept in through an 8-foot-wide Roman arched window facing the street. The decor harked back to the days when people actually lived in living rooms. They sat down in comfortable chairs upholstered in dark red fabrics. Reproductions from the Pre-Raphaelite period hung on the walls.

"Thank you for seeing us, Mr. Scott," Traci said.

"Frankly, I'm not accustomed to talking with detectives," Scott said. "But if it helps catch this pernicious scam artist, I don't mind."

"Sorry, we know you've been interviewed once," Stiles said. "Another look, though, might help us in our investigation."

"Is there a Mrs. Scott, and did she lose her identity as well?" Traci asked.

"I've been a widowed man for some years, detective."

"We're sorry to hear that."

"In some ways I find life is simpler."

Stiles asked. "See anything odd, like a car down the alley or somebody snooping around?"

"I'm afraid not."

"Do you discard copies of other documents? Anything we might get a lead from?"

Sigh. "No, that was pretty much it."

"Can we take a look at the trash bin? Maybe something was overlooked."

"Surely." He led them through the kitchen and service porch to the garage. Two 32-gallon bins were against the wall, a black one for waste and a green one for recyclables.

"I assume you close the lids for pickup," Traci said.

"Correct. After pickup, the lids are usually left open."

She looked into the open bin. It was empty.

"You reported unauthorized ATM withdrawals," Stiles said. "Is there a particular ATM that you often use?"

"Yes. The one outside the B of A branch at Sunset and Van Ness. That's the one I always use."

"We'll check their security tapes. But most likely the thief used a different branch to withdraw cash, one where you aren't known by sight."

"I hope you nail this parasite. He's caused me a world of grief, I can tell you."

"I'm sure," Stiles said. "If it's any consolation, I doubt that he'll go to the well twice."

"Thanks for your help, Mr. Scott," Traci said.

Driving back to the station house, Stiles turned to Traci. "Okay, we didn't get much out of this. But are you thinking what I'm thinking?"

"That this sort of a scam fits Victor Krait to a T?"

"Exactly."

Again, an All Points Bulletin was issued, this time for homicide suspect Victor Krait now known as Calvin A. Scott, same Honda Civic LX, tag number 5NUV3884.

If at first you don't succeed, hang in there.

After the arrest of illegal arms dealer Federico Cruz (Topo) by the LAPD, the case was turned over to Justice Department prosecutors. Subsequently detective Ed Chase received a subpoena to appear as a witness in Cruz' preliminary hearing. This would take place at Edward R. Roybal Federal Courthouse on Temple Street in downtown L.A. The subpoena was specific—Case number, defendant's name, date, time, witnesses, courtroom, etc. — no wiggle room for a detective to get out of it.

On September 9 at 1025 hours, Chase reported to the Bailiff and signed in. He found a Federal ADA in the courtroom already setting up at the prosecution table.

"Hi, I'm Ed Chase, LAPD Hollywood," he said, offering his hand.

"Jay Kravitz. Thanks for coming. I've read the transcript of your interview of Cruz."

"So did Judge Pinchaud. She didn't waste a lot of time remanding him."

"We've got Judge Pugmire today. He's as tough a judge as any. So what have you got for me?"

Chase placed an oblong canvas carrier on the table. "This is a military assault rifle secured for evidence by the recovery team. It was among some 40 mil-spec SBRs found in Cruz' headquarters. And here's a semi-auto Glock pistol, one of 55 handguns that were seized."

"Pretty persuasive exhibits," Kravitz said.

Chase also plopped down a three-ring binder filled with photographs, each marked for evidence. "These are photos of all the various weapons, both single and together in one large display. And also photos of explosive materials—RDX, Semtex, dynamite sticks, you name it."

"You guys have been busy, haven't you."

"Whatever it takes to get blood suckers like Cruz off the street."

At this moment, Federico Cruz was brought in by the Bailiff, who escorted him to the defense table. Judge Pugmire, a bulky gray-haired man wearing Coke bottle glasses, swooped in from Chambers. The Bailiff introduced him and recited the defendant's name and case number. Chase looked over at Topo. He was cleaned up like a choir boy. No more bandido mustache, hair trimmed and slicked back, tattoos covered by a dark brown business suit. What a joke, Chase thought to himself.

"This hearing is now in session," Judge Pugmire began. "Prosecution?"

Kravitz rose. "Federal attorney Jay Kravitz, your honor."

"Welcome to the court. And Defense?"

"Max Tischler, your honor. Tenny, Tischler & Traub."

"Ah yes, we meet again."

Chase remembered Tischler from a previous case. He'd gotten a 20-year-old gangster into juvenile court by submitting a birth certificate his mother had come up with showing his age as 17. Such documents were readily available on the street.

"Let's get the ball rolling," Judge Pugmire said. "The question before us today is this: Can a valid case be made that defendant Federico Cruz has trafficked in illegal arms and munitions, and is an accessory in the attempted assassination of Los Angeles Police Department detective John Stiles."

Before Pugmire could continue, Tischler rose to state, "Your honor, before we waste any more court time, I move for a continuance."

Kravitz was on his feet. "Your honor, what is—"

"I'll handle it," Pugmire said. "On what basis do you move, attorney?"

"My client was verbally and physically abused by LAPD detectives during his interrogation. As a result he is experiencing severe headaches and other mental aberrations." Tischler produced a 9 x 12 manila envelope from his briefcase. "I submit this evaluation by a licensed psychologist to show—"

Pugmire cut him off. "Spare us the chapter and verse, counsellor. I grant a continuance of 30 days, during which the defendant shall remain in custody." He banged his gavel and exited to chambers.

Tischler had successfully employed gangland's favorite legal weapon—delay. The strategy was to proceed in like fashion with last minute briefs until the Feds dropped the charges. Chase walked to his car and headed for the 101 on-ramp.

16

Big meeting at Hollywood. John Luttwak called in his two available Homicide units for a review of Carina's statement. Stiles and Little, and Miller and Kazurian sat at the table with their usual laptops, case files, phones, pads and pens. Also present was Behavioral Sciences Division psychologist Diane Metz. The fact that she was now Luttwak's wife in no way tainted her qualifications.

Luttwak handed out printed sheets, and said, "This is in your case file, but we'll use these for now." The six cops took a moment to leaf through.

"As you no doubt know, Carina Parra was interviewed by Miller and Kazarian and ADA Jim Presley last week. During the questioning Carina was trapped in a number of lies and obfuscations. Eventually she was persuaded by Presley that she was in serious trouble and that the only way she could save herself was to come clean with us. She finally broke down and agreed to write out everything she knows. What we need to determine today is how much of her statement is true and how much isn't."

Luttwak turned a 3- by 4-foot easel card around to face the table.

"This is a blow-up of what she wrote."

LOS ANGELES POLICE DEPARTMENT
Hollywood Division 06/08/11 DR No. 2011-07-2981
SWORN TESTIMONY OF MS. CARINA PARRA

I am Carina Parra, the wife of Raphael Parra, who was shot dead by LAPD Detective Jack Stiles during a Bank Robbery. Victor Krait was the mastermind of the robbery. Victor was arrested by Stiles' partner, Detective Little. I knew nothing of this until I saw it on TV.

I admit that prior to these events, I had known Victor Krait, and he was my lover. Victor was very good at illusions. He convinced me of three things—that his arrest was a mistake, that he loved me, and that Detective Stiles shot Raphael in cold blood. I know now that none of this was true.

When Victor was released from prison, I was still in love with him. I helped him establish himself. I had sex with him and I lent him my car. At that time I also had a boyfriend, Raymondo Luna. Raymondo abused me, and I was afraid of him. He carried a big knife and made threats to cut me.

Victor said he was going to use Raymondo Luna to kill detective Stiles. Afterward, Victor and I would betray Raydo and testify against him. But it never worked out that way, as everybody knows.

At this point (not known to me), Victor changed his identity to Guy X. Terminus. Something I forgot to say is that Victor told me about his secret bank account in Zurich. That is where the money came from to pay Raymondo. I did not know what Raymondo would do with it, or when. It was to be in two payments—five thousand dollars before Stiles' death and five thousand after. The first five thousand I gave to Raymondo. I don't know what Victor did with the second five thousand.

Victor admitted to me that he shot the man who provided him with his X. Terminus documents. I had no idea who the man was or why Victor would kill him. Victor showed me a pistol. This may be how he intends to kill Detective Stiles. I continued to see Victor and had sex *with him several times. I began to realize that Victor had serious mental obsessions, and also that Detective Stiles fired in the line of duty.*

Victor never mentioned anyone named Calvin Scott. The last time I saw Victor I had sex with him in a rented van. He will kill in cold blood at any time. I am in fear of my life as I write this.

(signed) *Carina Parra*

After they carefully reviewed the statement, Luttwak asked for comments.

"I want to go first," Traci said. "Before we get into this, let's cut Carina a little slack. She has made a series of bad mistakes in life—everything from a bad choice in marriage, to bad boyfriends, to allowing herself to be involved with a convicted criminal—and she's paid dearly for all of it. She isn't evil, Victor Krait is evil. She's just trying to save herself."

This tweaked Kazurian's Crimean genes. "Carina Parra is up to her neck in this. I've questioned plenty of suspects, and she lies like a Persian rug. Two murders have occurred and another failed. No way should we believe any bullshit from her."

Traci said, "That sexy Latina knows more than she's telling, but we've already got the basics. Why make her suffer for what that killer has done?"

"How about you, Irv?" Luttwak said. "You were there when she wrote this."

"I'm with my usual view, that persuasion will get you more results than abuse."

"Once in a while, maybe," Kaz said.

"Let's get back to the statement itself." Stiles said. "What parts of it are true and what parts aren't. Diane is a psychologist. If anyone can tell, she can."

Diane Metz spoke, and with evident authority.

"The truth is malleable, depending on who you are. To some people lying is difficult, to others it's a way of life. A habitual liar will lie saying Hello. Honesty depends mostly on genetics. Being around honest people may help, but generally you can't overcome a deep propensity to lie.

"Then there are the dissemblers. They tend to skirt the issue by changing the subject. If you confront them with an undeniable fact, they might say, 'Hey, your fingernails are dirty.' Something similar happens with traffic tickets. The driver will say, 'but that other guy was going faster than me.'

"Looking at Ms. Parra's statement, I would say that most of it is true. I get the impression that she wants to come clean. But to say that she knew nothing of the bank robbery is a stretch. I think her denial that she knew about Krait's Guy X. Terminus alias may be true. That she didn't know what Raymondo Luna would do with the money and when, however, is pure rubbish. I think she denied that out of fear.

"To say she didn't know what Victor did with the second five thousand is also a lie. All ten thousand went through her to Raymondo Luna, and she knows what happened to the rest of it. It's probably somewhere in her house. In fact, I consider it grounds for a search warrant of Ms. Parra's residence. Our justification could be to look for the gun that killed Crawley. As for his assuming the identity of Calvin Scott, I think Krait was under sufficient pressure that he might not have told her about it."

All of which might be right, but it didn't help locate Krait.

17

At the end of his 12-hour shift, Irv Miller logged out with the Watch Commander. He walked to the front end of the parking lot and unlocked his personal CRV. It was stuffy in the vehicle, which had been parked in the sun all day. He started the engine and turned the climate control selector to 68 degrees. Just then his cell chirped. He heard the cheerful voice of Rachel.

"Hi, hon, how was it today?"

"Not too bad. We're still looking for that psycho Victor Krait, though. It's amazing how slippery that crudball is. I'll tell you about it when I get home."

"Okay. Listen, I didn't get a chance to cook today. Can you stop at the deli?"

"Sure, no problem."

"Get whatever sandwich you want. I want some blintzes and sour cream, okay? And a quarter pound of chicken liver."

"Got it. I'll be there in about half an hour."

"Okay. I'll uncork a bottle of Merlot."

Things were always okay between Irv and Rachel. He knew she would want blintzes and she knew he'd get himself a pastrami sandwich. How many years was it that they'd been married? He couldn't remember the date. Like a lot of other stuff, he'd leave it to her. His brain was too full of cop work, and the serious issues of crime.

Miller headed west to Fairfax and entered Katz's Deli. Immediately he sensed that something was wrong. Three other customers were at a side counter looking scared. The counter man's voice quavered when he spoke.

"Hey, Irv. Where you been?"

"Other places, Larry. Stuck with no-taste white bread."

Then Miller saw the problem, a heavily inked 18-year-old gang member waving a Saturday night special. Miller could see he was high on meth.

"Everybody stay cool!" the man rasped. "Open the cash drawer and gimme the paper money!" He threw a bag on the counter. The bag didn't quite make it and slipped to the floor. All eyes went to the bag.

Miller reached inside his jacket for his Baretta, and shouted "LAPD! Drop your gun! Keep your hands where I can see them!" Instead the gangster swung his weapon in Miller's direction. Miller fired twice and the man fell to the floor bleeding profusely from his chest. Miller kicked his gun away and cuffed him. This proved to be unnecessary, for the man was already dead.

Sighs of relief and gratitude went through the room.

"Folks, this is my friend and steady customer, detective Irv Miller," Larry said. "Irv, you get free food for a year."

"Works for me," Miller said. He called Hollywood station on his cell phone: Off-duty detective 8W65 confronted with 211 suspect, location 1642 N. Fairfax Ave, firearms discharged, suspect down, request paramedics and patrol backup. In a few minutes an ambulance and two black and whites arrived and secured the area. Miller called Rachel and told her it would be a while. In fact it was 8AM the next morning before he got home.

"Sorry I'm so late, hon," he said, unstrapping his gear and putting it on the buffet.

Rachel gave him a nice kiss and handed him a glass of orange juice. "What happened?" she asked.

"I walked into a holdup at the deli and I had to shoot the suspect. So now I'll have to appear before the Shooting Review Board."

That was okay with Rachel. "At least you came home in one entire piece," she said.

The weekend arrived. Detective team 1 had Saturday off. This morning, as Traci sat in her nook eating fruity yogurt and looking out the window, her cell twittered. She took it leaning against the counter.

"Wake up, detective," Stiles said.

"I've been up over an hour, dear. You know that."

"Wait till I show you what I just bought."

"An Uzbeki mountain goat?"

"A different animal, one with four wheels and a V-8."

She stood up straight. "You bought a Mustang?"

"Right, a convertible. A red one."

"My favorite color. Where are you going to take me?"

"How about a trip up the coast on the PCH?"

"Terrific, I can't wait."

Traci spent the morning shopping for a new bikini. She found one in silver. Also a hot pink nylon cover for the midday sun. Jack liked hot colors, she knew. She tied her hair back into a ponytail, perfect for an open ride. Stiles stuck with his usual format, cargo shorts, T-shirt and shades. He threw his kit and his shotgun into the trunk, lowered the top and drove to Traci's condo at two o'clock. She was waiting out front, sitting on a low garden wall. She hopped into the Mustang traveling light—bikini, nylon cover, no shoes, no wallet, no keys, no money.

She said, "Hi," and settled on beige leather.

Stiles took the 10 to Pacific Coast Highway and turned north. The Mustang responded with ease, the throaty sound of its engine rising like an anthem.

"I so love this car," Traci told him. "It's so cool, so fast, so sexy."

"Matches up nicely with you."

"I guess that makes me a Mustang girl. They're very sexy, in case you didn't know."

"I've seen the website. Girls in teeny bikinis crawling all over them."

"A tradition I fully intend to live up to."

"Is that a promise?"

"Yes."

Passing Sunset, Traci said, "You know, the best thing about this is, it makes you completely forget about the job, about Victor Krait and all the other wing-dings out there causing grief."

"Right on. This is our day, all 250 miles of it."

The Mustang sped forward, past beach houses along the shore, past Topanga Canyon and Las Flores, on through Malibu and a few small shoreline beach towns. Traffic was moving along reasonably well for a summer weekend. The weather was warm, with a seductive on-shore breeze. Santa Cruz Island rose dimly in the distance.

Passing Point Mugu, two Navy F/A-18 Hornets thundered directly overhead on final decent to the Naval Base.

Traci was stoked. "Geez Louise, what a blast!"

"Just be happy they're ours," Stiles said.

Stiles exited west on Point Hueneme Road all the way to Channel Islands harbor and marina. Traffic slowed along the shoreline, with its pretty inlets and beaches. They stopped for some wine and sauteed scallops at a little restaurant along the shore. From their table on the deck, they had a fine view of the beach and the breakers rolling in. The sound had a calming effect after the two jets.

"This is nice." Traci said. "Did you know about this place?"

"No, just dumb luck."

Traci spotted some sandpipers. "Look at those little pointy-beaked birds scooting back and forth between waves."

"Looking for sand crabs, I reckon."

"They all look identical, but there's one that's always the first to run up the shore and the first to run back."

"Even a flock of shorebirds has its leader."

"Just like in the Department."

"Today I don't want to hear nothin' about no Department."

"Look, they're so cute, poking their beaks in there like little skewers."

"Maybe you better ask a sand crab."

Stiles paid up and they took a little walk along the shore.

Traci sighed. "God, it's so great to be up here, so far from the usual stuff we do every day."

"No gangsters, no loonies."

"No child abusers."

"Don't remind me."

"Just normal people, the ones we serve and protect. It just feels flat out wonderful."

That was it for the north tour. Stiles accessed PCH again and headed for home. The ocean was on their right now, the sun twenty degrees off the horizon. The air was tropical and the light was rosy. No need for the nylon cover-up now. Traci tossed it and released her ponytail from its clasp. She lay back with her eyes closed, catching the late rays.

Stiles glanced over at her, loving the image.

"You look terrific in that silver outfit," he said. "Like a space girl from the planet Venus."

A smile, eyes closed. "Calling this an outfit is something of a stretch."

"I wonder what Uptight McKnight would do if he could see you right now."

She laughed. "He'd jack off. Then he'd try to blackmail me into having sex with him. I'd tell him to get stuffed or I'd sue him for sexual harassment."

"Not a bad idea."

She waved at the driver of a truck they were passing and got a horn blast and a thumbs up in return.

A few more miles, a few more trucks, a few more waves and traffic began to slow. Beach towns were beginning to pop up now, and surfers were crossing the highway to get to their cars. After Malibu, Traci put her nylon cover back on.

"Wow, this trip has been majorly fun, detective," she said.

Stiles thought so too. "Especially due to you and your sexy fashion show."

"You think? Wait till you see our Mustang photo crawl."

"You're really going to do that?"

"Absolutely."

Stiles turned off at Sunset and took the scenic route to Hollywood. Back to reality. Back to chasing Victor Krait and other assorted misanthropes. Back to frustration, success, triumphs, death and tears. Back to life according to the Job.

18

Irv Miller sighed and tore open the envelope with his copy of the LAPD Shooting Review Board's findings, a document that could be crucial to the continued success (or lack of it) of his career. This is what he read:

LOS ANGELES POLICE DEPARTMENT
SHOOTING REVIEW BOARD
OFFICER-INVOLVED SHOOTING

DIVISION; HWD   DATE: 8/08/2011   DUTY: OFF   IN UNIFORM? NO

OFFICER INVOLVED: DET. I IRVING L. MILLER   LENGTH SERV: 13 YRS, 7 MONTHS

SUBJECT: EDUARDO RINCONE   M, AGE 22 (EST.)   DECEASED.

REASON FOR POLICE CONTACT:

Detective Miller entered a food establishment with a robbery in progress. Subject was armed with a semi-automatic pistol, holding counter man and 3 patrons at gunpoint. Detective Miller, having served 7 years in drug enforcement, recognized Subject's symptoms of amphetamine inducement. Subject demanded contents of cash drawer.

Subject was momentarily distracted by dropping his money bag. Detective Miller drew his service weapon, identified himself as a Police officer, and ordered Subject to drop his weapon. Subject failed to comply, pointing his weapon at Detective Miller.

In fear of his life, and the lives of others, Detective Miller fired two rounds at Subject, killing him. Detective Miller forthwith radioed Hollywood Division

Station reporting the incident and requesting assistance. Other persons present were not injured. Field Unit analysis confirms Detective Miller's account of events as they transpired as accurate. Serology Unit, through postmortem examination, confirms the presence of methamphetamine in subject's blood.

LOS ANGELES POLICE DEPARTMENT SHOOTING REVIEW BOARD FINDINGS

A. Tactics:
   Considering the situation at the time of occurrence, The SRB finds Detective Miller's tactics to be appropriate, justified, and within LAPD Operational Rules and Procedures.
B. Drawing, Exhibiting, Holstering:
   The SRB finds Det. Miller's drawing to be within OR&P requirements.
C. Use of force:
   The SRB finds Det. Miller's use of force to be justified and within OR&P.

Andrea Gorshin   Secretary, Shooting Review Board

Dick Cheevers knocked on John Luttwak's office door.

"I just got the news. Judge Pinchaud has issued a court order granting a search of Carina Parra's house."

"Wonderful. That tough old bird has her head screwed on right."

"I hope some scabby lawyer isn't going to challenge the fruit of the search."

"I don't care, as long as it helps us find Victor Krait. We've got plenty of other evidence to arrest and convict him with."

"I'll believe it when I see it."

"Get a copy of the warrant. Meanwhile I'm through with wasting you and Chase on surveillance. An undercover unit can do that. When the warrant comes, you two will handle the search. I'll call up a couple of black and whites to do the heavy lifting."

"Okay. I'll round up Ed and wait for your go."

"Play it safe. It's conceivable that Krait might be there, and we know what he's capable of."

That functional psychopath was not pleased with the way things were going. Victor Krait had sufficient money and resources, but for one reason or another he was no closer to destroying Jack Stiles. He would not be satisfied with simply walking up to him and firing off a couple of shots. It had to be dramatic, even spectacular. Stiles must be blasted, torn, dismembered, blown away, or something of the sort. And if others cops died with him, so much the better

Another thing that racked him was his growing suspicion that Carina was informing on him. She must have sneaked a look at his drivers license. How else could the cops discover his newest identity? he asked himself.

He began to follow her during her various trips to clothing boutiques, latin food markets, aromatherapy sessions, coffee with girlfriends, and so forth. It was such a pleasure to photograph her through the zoom lens of his camera, knowing that this star-quality Latina was his to play with. Imagine his shock, when on one such mission he saw her park on Wilcox Avenue and enter the Hollywood station. His beautiful Latina, whose luscious body he feasted on, was talking to the police. About him.

The Full Clip was brimming with cops the night of Luttwak's and Diane's first anniversary, especially from Hollywood and Rampart Divisions. High-ranking brass from Central, supervisors, detectives, patrol officers, gang task force members, field unit techs, ADAs and staffers were all there in force.

John and Diane sat at the head table with people they most respected and worked with every day, including Jack Stiles, Irv Miller, Dick Cheevers and Ed Chase. Kazurian was in San Diego testifying in a murder trial. Traci walked in wearing a cami and shorts. No formality in this crowd. Stiles got up from the table and offered Traci his seat. He leaned against the bar with a half pint of Sam Adams.

Dick Cheevers got up from the head table and clinked a fork against a double shooter glass with I♥LA on it. The recorded music was muted.

"Ladies and gentlemen, and all you other people." Hoots and laughs. "It's my privilege to present to you the honorees of the hour, John and Diane Luttwak." Cheers, applause. "You may know them as the renown but nosy Lieutenant of the Detectives table, as well as the salad, roast beef, and dessert tables," Laughter. "and his charming wife Diane." Cheers and applause.

"Now many of you folks will remember her as Diane Metz," Cheevers went on, "from the Department's Behavioral Sciences Division. Those are the ones with white coats and rubber gloves who wanna put you in the loony bin." Hoots and boos.

"But Diane isn't like that. Depending on your gender, she hypnotize you, give you dreams about men with good abs, and loose women—you've heard of Righty Tighty and Lefty Lucy?

"But I digress. Lieutenant married her because now if he wants a psych report, he can just roll over in bed." Laughter and hoots. "Look at her laughing. She ain't sleeping in the garage, right?" Laughs, cheers.

"Now Wak, he's been a lot easier to get along with. Use to be he'd send us to the I-A cops when we were bad." Hoots and boos. "Now he only hangs us by our thumbs in the lobby. You guys with the sore thumbs, think how much worse it could be." Laughter.

Cheevers paused for a swig of beer.

"Now we get to the sentimental part. John and Diane, we know how lucky we are to have a pair like you callin' the shots. We'll stand by you, and when the chips are down we'll back you up all the way. Everybody—every man and woman crammed into this place for honest cops, raise your glass." The room hushed.

"Here's to two fine police officers and two good friends of all of us."

Glasses all across the room were guzzled and drained. Cheerful jazz music from the bar's audio system started up, and The Clip became a noisy brotherly bar again. Some people went to the table to shake hands with Luttwak and Diane. Others returned to the bar and their usual cop talk.

19

At night, dressed from head to toe in black, Krait approached Carina's house through an alleyway. The blinds were closed but interior light showed through. It was only after two hours of quiet and dim night lights, that he noticed the two men in a van across the street from the house. This confirmed his suspicion that Carina was betraying him.

Krait's response to that was to out-wait the watchers. Finally, at 3AM, the van drove away. He waited a few minutes more, then rapped on the back door. Nothing. He rapped again and Carina's voice said, "Who is it?"

"Victor."

She opened the door to him. "Victor, I'm thrilled to see you, but why so late?"

"The police are watching your house."

"Why would they do that?"

"To find me, obviously. You've been talking to them, haven't you."

She brushed this aside. "Come to the living room where we can see by the light of the wall sconces." She took his hand and guided him to the brighter room.

"Answer my question please," he persisted.

"No, of course I haven't."

Krait produced Miller's business card. "Don't lie to me,

Carina. It isn't becoming."

Her face went ashen. "Where did you get that?"

"From your purse. There is nothing you can hide from me, my love."

"All right, so the police did question me. But I told them nothing."

"Do they know about Calvin Scott?"

"Who is that?"

"I believe you know full well, princesa, but let it pass for the moment."

Krait freed the semi-auto from his belt and placed it on the coffee table. He drew Carina to him and kissed her face and throat.

"This is so romantic," she breathed, "Coming to me in the night like an archangel,"

"As it is written."

"Would you like some Rioja?" she asked.

"Perhaps a little."

She poured a glass of the wine and they both drank from it as they embraced.

Her voice came as a whisper. "Fuck me, querido."

"Of course, my darling. But first I must ask you what you did with the five thousand dollars that was set aside for Raymondo's second payment?"

"Don't worry. It's hidden so cleverly that even you couldn't find it."

Krait was not pleased with this obfuscation. "If I should need it, tell me now."

"It's better that you don't know, in case—"

"Why are you playing games with me, Carina?"

She laughed. "In case you run off with some cock teaser."

Krait realized that he wasn't going to get an answer, so he might as well enjoy what he had planned to do.

He pulled her baby doll over her head and made himself naked. Together they sank to the carpet in an urgent melding of flesh.

"Hurry, querido."

"This will be a night to remember," Krait said. "I promise you that."

The quality of sex that ensued was particularly exquisite for Krait, because he well knew what was to follow. Leaving Carina lying breathless, he went to the table and recovered his pistol. He drew the silencer from his jacket and began screwing it onto the barrel.

"What are you doing, Victor?" she cried, eyes wide open.

"Keeping you from ratting to the cops."

He chugged three rounds into Carina's upper body. Blood spurted from her in a single pulse and then simply pooled on the carpet. Krait dressed again. He put the gun and the silencer in his jacket. What a pity, he thought. So beautiful, yet so unfaithful. With a kitchen rag, he wiped the wine glass clean. After making a fruitless search for the money, he walked away into the night.

John Luttwak's plans for a search of Carina Parr's residence were temporarily shelved. A new sweep of the Alvarados gang was being prepared. This virulent Latino street gang, backed by the Mexican Mafia, controlled large areas of Highland Park, Glassell Park, Cypress Park and two other downtown neighborhoods.

An earlier raid against the Alvarados by a task force formed by the U. S. Drug Enforcement Administration, the LAPD, and other jurisdictions had been highly successful. 88 gang members were taken into custody. Charges included murder, robbery, extortion, auto theft, and drug trafficking. In the process, large quantities of drugs, money and weapons were recovered.

After several years of relative decline, the Alvarados were again rampant and out of control. A new multi-agency task force was about to strike. Hollywood Division's homicide, robbery, burglary, autos, drugs, and anti-gang units, along with hundreds of patrol officers, would participate.

Luttwak briefed his squad leaders in the station house conference room.

"Most of us have participated in these gang sweeps before. Now we're going to put together one of the largest ever, under the code name Urban Legend. Total forces will number more than 1, 200 armed officers, including all available personnel on the day of the raid. Warrants are being prepared as we speak.

"The operation is scheduled for Wednesday, August 15th, at 0400 hours. DEA will assume overall command. Check out vests, shotguns, and assault rifles from the Kit Room as needed. Staging area will be Dodger Stadium parking lot a half-hour prior.

"Even though we'll be taking these gangsters by surprise, remember they're still armed and dangerous. Make sure your people know where they are, relative to where other officers are positioned. You may be fired on at any time. Last, be sure to observe LAPD Operational Rules and Procedures. We don't want any legal screw-ups that we'll regret later.

"Operation Urban Legend is detailed in this written briefing. It's also in your lap-tops under the Inter-Agency Operations file, Section 2."

Luttwak handed out 12-page summaries, then took questions.

Stiles and Little were assigned an address in East Hollywood. They arrived in a pool car, the same make as a patrol car, but painted generic brown. They met with two P/O units a block down the street to plan their approach and wait for the Go signal. Stiles carried a shotgun and Traci carried her 9mm Glock. Both had flashlights to use in the pre-dawn light

At last the green light was given. Nothing was stirring inside the house. Four of the officers took the front and two covered the back. Stiles covered the garage area, and Traci took the kitchen door and porte cochère where a Toyota sedan was parked.

One of the P/Os shouted, "Police! Arrest warrant! Open up!" Without waiting for a response, another officer hit the door with a battering ram and burst the lock out of the frame. The raiders entered with guns drawn, rousting four tattooed gangsters out of bed. A half-naked Latina screamed and ran into the bathroom. The four men were lined up, cuffed and searched.

In the driveway, one shaved-dome cholo burst out of the kitchen with keys, trying for the car. Traci aimed her weapon at him with a steady two-hand grip. "Police! Turn around and put your hands on your head and spread your legs apart!"

He was slow to comply. "Hey, Ladee, you goin' to shoot me? I don't think so."

Traci would love to have handled it herself, but she followed procedure. Using her left hand she called Stiles' cell. "Got one in the driveway. Non-cooperative, request assistance."

The gangster was getting restive. He took his hands down and faced her, taunting her with a laugh.

"Hey El-A-Pee-Dee girl, you shoot me, you end up in jail. You think you can cuff me? Go ahead."

"Turn around and face the wall! Do it now!"

His eyes glanced to the side, measuring the distance to the vehicle's door. "Go for it, bad boy," Traci said. "You run, I open fire."

Stiles arrived, in black like a messenger of death. He body-slammed the gangster against the wall, brought him down, and pressed his Baretta to the back of his neck. The cholo chose the easy way—short jail term, probation, him and his homies back on the street again. Traci took her handcuffs from her belt and snapped them on his wrists with practiced skill. Her Academy instructor's warning had sunk in. "If you're going to cuff somebody, do it fast."

"I'll take care of this guy," Stiles said. "You're wanted inside. There's a scared Latina in the bathroom that's about to be rammed open. She'll need a female officer."

The task force sweep was a success by any measure—44 Avenues members arrested on existing warrants for unsolved murders, armed robberies, drug dealing and other serious crimes. 51 additional arrests were made on related charges at the scene. Gangsters were hauled off to Rampart Station and shackled to long benches like army grunts at a latrine.

Materials recovered during the sweep included 10 kilos of black tar heroin from Tialchapa, 28 kilos of crystal meth and other drugs, over $40,000 in U.S. currency, garages full of stolen property (most in the original packaging), armaments, including handguns, assault rifles and 1,000 rounds of ammunition.

20

With his attention now focused on the extermination of Jack Stiles, Victor Krait began to seek the right weapon to carry it out. He suspected that military firearms were available on-line, and he was right. At a local internet cafe, he accessed the Allegheni Firearms Co. site and found a gallery of 15 military assault weapons, from Russian AK-47s to Israeli UZIs, all legally modified for civilian use.

He found a Colt Commando Short Barrel Rifle that would fit his needs, but the site required valid ID, numerous State and Federal approval forms, and a thirty-day wait. This was both frustrating and sobering—sobering because it reminded him that his Calvin Scott persona could be broken by the slightest misstep. Frustrating because now he would have to buy an assault weapon on the street. So be it, he decided. He'd faced worse in his life. It hadn't stopped him so far, and it wouldn't stop him now.

He started in the barrios of East L. A. The lack of city services was evident in the potholed streets, the run-down parks, and the clusters of idle youths hanging out by mini-markets and fast food places. Every decent-sized wall was tagged with graffiti, mostly gang signs. Krait's northern european looks didn't fit the scene here, but he persevered.

Spotting three young Latinos in undershirts and baggy pants in front of a taco stand, Krait pulled to the curb. One of them leaned on the passenger window sill.

"You wan' something, mister?"

"I need a little information," Krait said.

"You look like a fuckin' cop to me."

"If I was, I wouldn't come here alone."

The man looked up and down the street and saw nothing.

"Okay, so wha' you need?"

"I've got a hundred bucks for anyone who can take me to a weapons dealer. I'm not talking about a store."

The Latino went to his homies and talked it over in Spanish. He pulled out a phone and made a call. Returning to Krait, he said, "I do this for you, but the money is up front."

"Deal. Get in the car." Krait placed a pair of $50 bills in the cup holder.

A circuitous drive though downtown streets, guided by cell phone calls, ended at a small cafe on Cypress Avenue. Krait pulled to the curb in front. The cholo seized the two fifties and got out. "The man you wan' is near the back. His name is Sorbo."

Krait fed the parking meter and entered. At a table near the kitchen he could see a gray-haired man with a high forehead and rimless spectacles drinking a glass of red wine and reading a Serbian newspaper. He was the only light-skinned person in the cafe.

Krait drew up a chair. "Mr. Sorbo, I presume."

"That is so."

"My name is Calvin Scott. You were highly recommended to me."

Sorbo folded his newspaper. "Will you join me in a glass of Madero? It is the closest to Balkan red that is obtainable here."

"Thank you, I will."

Sorbo signaled a waiter and a glass of wine appeared. Krait raised his glass. "You know, in the barrio I'm surprised to be talking to an eastern European."

"Ancestry is meaningless in my trade. In fact, Latino street gangs are my most frequent clients."

"I see no reason to doubt it."

Sorbo cut to the chase.

"So, I am told that you require certain ordnance."

"Correct. For a personal matter. I want to purchase a Colt Commando SBR."

"A powerful weapon. We don't deal in Colt, but you can order one on-line at two or three different sites."

"I would, except there are paperwork problems and a 30 day wait. My need is immediate. With you, of course, I will pay in U.S. currency."

"I see." Sorbo took a look at Krait through his cerulean eyes, rating him as a dilettante. "What I can do, Mr. Scott, is supply you with a Bushmaster 5.56mm M4 semiautomatic rifle, a NATO mil-spec assault weapon. It is light but powerful, with a modified 12" barrel and 6-position butt stock. It fires 20 rounds per magazine."

"What about sighting?"

"It comes with a dual aperture M16A2 optics. If you want to add an infra-red night vision upgrade, you can find that at any gun store."

"What is the price, including an extra magazine and 200 rounds of ammunition?"

"Because a short barrel is illegal the price will be $4,500. The A2 optics are another $500. The rest is trivial. I throw it in."

"When?"

"You can pick it up tomorrow at 10 PM in the parking lot behind the cafe."

"Excellent."

How easy that was, thought Krait as he drove away.

Armed with the search warrant, Dick Cheevers and Ed Chase met with two patrol units down the street from Carina's house. The detectives and the patrol officers settled on a game plan for the search. They approached on foot with the P/Os taking the point.

Outwardly they saw nothing to imply Victor Krait's presence, nevertheless their hands were on their weapons. Two officers checked out the site, noting Carina's car sitting silently in the side driveway with its hood cold. All was quiet.

Cheevers and Chase stood aside, while the uniformed cops looked in the windows. Through the blinds one of the P/Os saw something. "God, it looks like a dead woman on the floor."

Cheevers looked too. "Damn, you're right."

Wasting no time, they broke the door in, and confirmed what they'd seen. Cheevers quickly identified the body as being Carina Parra. A search for any other bodies or live occupants was carried out. Cheevers radioed the situation to Hollywood and requested that Lieutenant Luttwak call his cell phone. Moments later Luttwak replied.

"What've you got, Dick?"

"Carina Parra is dead on the rug at her house."

"God have mercy. Are you certain she's really dead?"

"Yeah. Three holes in her upper body and blood all over the place."

"Krait has to be the shooter, just to shut her up."

"Her nightie is on the floor nearby, so she may have been raped."

"The coroner will figure it out. I'm sending you backup, and some techs to do their dust and scrape act."

"Okay. Ed and I recovered a wine glass. Why only one, I'm wondering."

"Maybe Krait took his with him."

"Maybe so. Anyway, after things are secured, we'll do what we came for—search the place."

Luttwak's usual phlegmatic view gave way. "Damn, I hate to see this. She was deep into it, but she didn't deserve this."

"I know. What a terrible waste."

Patrol cars started arriving and a perimeter was established. The first unit started a crime scene log—who came and when. The two detectives recorded what they observed from the death scene, and kept everybody else out until the Field Unit arrived. Then they began their previously assigned search of the house.

Every closet, every dresser drawer, every sofa cushion, every picture frame was examined for signs of Victor Krait. In the kitchen they found Carina's cell phone and bagged it for evidence. They checked the oven, the dishwasher, under the sink. A crew would handle the drains and electrical fixtures. In the pantry they found five thousand dollars stashed in a flour canister.

21

Traci recognized her sister's ringtone and picked up.

"Hi, Liz. What's up?"

"Not a whole lot. Just that I haven't heard from you lately."

"Sorry, we've been majorly busy. How's your CPA operation going?"

"Slow. It always is in summer. But it'll pick up in the fall. My clients will be trying to figure out the new IRS rules and want to work out a strategy for coping with them. By December they'll be hysterical. I do love working for myself, that I'll say. So what's going down at Hollywood?"

"There was a horrible shooting this week. A beautiful Latina. She was a key witness we've been interviewing. Our guys were serving a search warrant at her place and found her on floor, shot to death."

"How horrible. Do you know who did it?"

"We think so. There was sperm in her, but we don't have the guy to match it to."

"That must drive you crazy."

"Crazy is the name of the game in police work."

"You know, I still can't get over you being homicide cop—my sister the crime buster, running around with a pistol on her belt. I'm glad to know it wasn't you that got shot."

Traci reassured. "No way, with Jack Stiles backing me up."

"So how is that good-looking rascal these days?"

"Real fine. Actually Jack's the reason I wanted to talk to you. Kim and I are meeting for lunch at Cinzano's, and Jack will be the main subject. Want to join us?"

"Sure. What time?"

"12: 15. There's usually parking on the street."

Cinzano's had nothing to do with the Vermouth bottler, but they had umbrellas with the name and the waiters wore green aprons. Traci and Liz were at a table when Kim Kaelin walked in. Kim was a streaky blonde about Traci's age with clear blue eyes. She and Traci had come up together at the Academy and had kept in touch ever since. Kim now worked in LAPD Records and Identification Division, aka Records.

"Hi, you two," she greeted, and unslung her tote bag. "Liz, it's been a while. You're looking gorgeous, I must say."

"What I was thinking about you, girl."

A waiter approached and Liz and Kim ordered martinis. Traci wasn't supposed to drink on duty, but she ordered one anyway.

Kim said, "I love this place, don't you?"

"So do the studio people," Traci said. "Don't look now, there's Steve Carell just behind you."

"Oh, I love him."

"Don't get your panties in a twist. He's with Nancy."

"Aw shit."

Kim leaped to the main subject. "So. How's your partner these days?"

"Jack's fine."

"Fine? Where's the heat? Where's the passion?"

Traci went confidential. "Swear you never heard any of this, or I'll have to kill you."

"Scout's honor, it's safe with us."

"Okay. Profile of detective Jack Stiles: Grade A sexy, and doesn't even know it. You should see him naked. Every square inch of him is solid. His only flaw is a scar on his left shoulder from taking down a guy waving a buck knife. When Jack and I are alone, all rational thought evaporates. I just can't keep my fingerprints off of him."

"Lucky girl," Liz said. "Between the two of us, God made you for him. And he made you blond too."

"I'll tell you something else. Jack's a hell of a cop. Any frootloop out there that pulls a gun on Jack is dead before he hits the asphalt."

"That good, huh?" Kim said.

"Believe it. At the range his score is 392. A perfect score is 400, which means 40 rounds in the 10 ring."

"Yeesh. I'm starting to feel sorry for the bad guys."

The martinis arrived and all three ordered salads.

Liz was waiting for the big news. "Traci, what's with Jack that calls us here today? Is something going on?"

"Okay. First of all, Jack's coupe got blown up—"

"We know that."

"Well, he went out and bought a Mustang convertible."

Kim was stoked. "Ohh, I love that car."

"Me too," Liz said. "There's always a kind of mystique about a Mustang."

"This one is red, and it's fast, and it's totally sexy."

"That's by definition."

"Jack and I took a test run up the coast to the Channel Islands marina. We had lunch and drinks at a little place along the shore. It was warm and breezy, just beautiful. It put me in a wonderful mood."

Traci guzzled her drink and went on.

"I'd worn a bikini that day and a nylon cover up. On the return trip the sun was sinking and the light was starting to get that rosy glow. I was feeling fabulous and free. When we passed Point Mugu, I tossed the cover. No need for sun protection any more. God, the breeze felt so wonderful and refreshing. I felt an irresistible urge to go topless. Why not? Only two tiny wisps of cloth were in the way."

"Outrageous," Liz laughed. "I can see the tabloids now."

"Exactly. If Jack and I were pulled over, there would've been a terrible scandal. All sorts of bad things would happen and Lieutenant Luttwak would suffer for it. So I decided some other time, some other place."

"Of which, may there be many."

After a martini pause, Traci came to the point.

"Anyway, here's what I want to talk to you about. I want to inaugurate Jack's Mustang with a little photo session. What I have in mind is a sexy photo crawl, and I need you two to make it a triple feature."

"Hey, what a cool idea," Kim said.

"And you'd be perfect for it. You're both totally gorgeous."

"So who else will be there?"

"Maybe Jack's friend Ted Redfern."

"Oh my god," Kim said. "I've got such a crush on him. He always flirts when he calls me at Records. And now he has my cell number. When he calls me at night the dialogue definitely heats up."

"Well, here's your chance to show him what you own."

"I definitely will do that."

Liz to Traci, "You sure you want us wiggling our ass for your guy?"

"Don't be silly. This is the twenty-first century."

"What'll we do with the pictures?"

"I don't know. Dig 'em out when we're feeling blue. Save them for our grandchildren."

"Look, here's Grammy when she was hot!"

All three laughed. "That works," Traci said. "The main idea is to run loose and show some skin. C'mon, it'll be a lot of fun."

"What about security?"

"Not to worry. We'll be doing this somewhere out in the boonies."

"Okay, I'm up for it," Liz said. "I'll bring my Nikon."

Kim drained her glass. "I'm so there."

"Terrific. The three of us will christen Jack's Mustang like he never dreamed of."

22

John Luttwak met with his detectives working the latest of Krait's cold-blooded murders. It was frustrating that the man still eluded them with such seeming ease. They sat down at the table with their usual laptops, case files, coffee, doughnuts and the like. The mood was subdued.

"What's in Carina's cell phone, Dick? Anything that we can use?"

"Yeah, some recent calls from Krait on Calvin Scott's AT&T account. The company won't give us dialogue, but they'll give us locations if the caller is within range of three cell towers. In this case AT&T gave us frequent calls from within shouting distance of 3rd and Fairfax. Others were around West Hollywood shopping areas along Beverly, just as you might expect."

"Recent texting was still in the phone's memory," Chase said, handing out transcripts.

After glancing through, Stiles said, "Pretty heavy on sex, but no cigar."

"What about this?" Cheevers said. "I LUV YR FUZ AGNST MY CHEEK. Sounds like the guy is growing a beard. And here where she texts U LK SO DSTINGWISHT. Just what we need—a diplomatic killer."

"Fine," Luttwak said. "We'll photoshop a beard on him and release it to the media."

"One text from him says, GOT NU TAGS. COPS L NVR FIND ME."

Tracy smiled like the Calico Cat. "Uh oh, not so fast, Victor. A bulletin came in this morning that just might suggest the contrary."

"We wish," Stiles said.

"A couple of hikers found a Chevy sedan in a canyon below Mulholland Drive in Sherman Oaks. It looked too good to be a junker, so they reported it. The car had no license tags, but the VIN was 503362044. We contacted the DMV. They say the license tag was 4STL2827. Guess who could be driving with those tags."

"Mr. Diplomacy in his Honda Civic," Cheevers said.

"It's a long shot, but it's worth another APB," Luttwak said. "Meanwhile, I like the 3rd and Fairfax locus. I'll issue an order to BOLO the car in that area. You guys check out the purchases on Calvin Scott's Visa card. We've got to nail that guy before he kills somebody else."

Miller and Kazurian ate lunch in West Hollywood. A favorite place for quick food was Pink's hot Dog Stand on La Brea near Melrose. Pink's was world famous but they never tried to go fancy. It was little more than a shack with a long window and a big sign that said CHILI DOGS. They were celebrating their 70th anniversary today and the line was long.

This was Kaz's first experience of Pink's. "I've heard that celebrities are in here all the time, but I don't see any right now, do you?"

"No, it's too crowded right now," Irv said. "But I saw Eddie Murphy in here the other day."

"You eat here often then?"

"Ever since I was transferred to Hollywood."

"You haven't lost any weight over it."

Irv laughed his dry laugh, a sound often tinged with irony. "That's the trouble with it. I'm addicted. When I die they'll find my veins clogged up with wieners."

The line moved and the smell of the hot dogs was stronger.

"What do you recommend?"

"The regular chili dog is the best. It's ten inches long and topped with chili, onions, sauerkraut, and real mustard. Not that yellow stuff."

Five minutes later they got their food, which actually took 30 seconds to prepare. They sat at an umbrella table they found on the Melrose side. Little brown birds were hopping back and forth picking up crumbs. Traffic was heavy on the boulevard. Cedars-Sinai Medical Center was a couple of blocks south and they heard an ambulance in the distance.

Kazurian said, "You know, Irv, this is another reason why I like being partnered with you. You know all the good places to grab a bite. In Armenia my family died for food, but all there was was beets and cabbage."

"That's what life is, man. Survival. Or just plain luck."

"Yeah, like getting lucky with a case. I read in the L.A. Times the other day about some putz that's been holed up in Chula Vista for three years, and finally got nailed because of a parking ticket. You believe it? One of the cops there was checking through the old BOLOs and recognized the tag number."

"We should be that lucky, Irv."

Three tables away a lightly bearded Victor Krait sat reading a copy of USA TODAY. Neither he nor the detectives were aware of the other.

Traci parked on the corner of Stiles' desk, looking over his shoulder while he printed out Calvin Scott's Visa statement.

"Macy's, Ralph Lauren, A/X, a dozen or so restaurant tabs," Stiles recited.

"Mostly in West Hollywood area, so what else is new," Traci said.

"Shit, no motels, no car lubes, a couple of cash withdrawals from that ATM Scott told us about. Krait must park someplace and walk over there."

"Look, here's an ordinary everyday plain folks purchase from Sammy's."

"Sammy's Camera?"

"No, Sammy's Guns and Ammo."

They found it on Moorpark in the Valley—a sorry-looking shack of a building with iron bars on all the doors and windows. Out front, the asphalt drive-up parking was two rows deep with muddy pickups and off-road vehicles. Jack's red Mustang stood out like a prom queen.

They were buzzed through a security door. Inside were long counters and showcases with revolvers and semi-automatics. Shotguns and look-alike assault rifles were racked up along the wall behind the counters.

"Help you, folks?" the inflated ruddy-faced proprietor said.

"LAPD," Stiles stated. They showed him their badges and ID wallets.

"Well, I'm the owner. Sammy ain't my real name, a course. But we're always ready to cooperate with the Law. What do you need to know?"

"We're investigating a homicide—"

"You mean this pretty girl here is a homicide cop?"

Traci smiled. "Yep."

"Well, I'll be a blue-nosed gopher."

"The suspect made a Visa card purchase recently," Stiles said. "The last four digits would be 8055."

"Has he got a name?"

"Calvin A. Scott."

"Oh yeah. I remember him. Tall, stubby beard, no way your typical tin can plunker.

"That fits. What we need to know is what he bought."

"No problem. Let me pull up the charge card file." Sammy pecked away at his laptop. "If it's the guy I'm thinkin' of he bought night vision optics for a short barrel rifle."

The printer made some whirry sounds and out poured six pages of card purchases for July and August. Sammy went down the lines with his ballpoint.

"Here it is. Infra red upgrade for M16A2 optics. That fits a whole passel of SBRs. I think he said Bushmaster."

That wasn't news a homicide cop likes to hear.

23

On their next weekend day off, Traci invited Stiles over for a late afternoon session on the roof. He pulled directly into the parking level entrance using a card Nathan had given him.

Stiles carried a thermos of chilled martinis and two plastic wine glasses. Traci's dupe key opened the third floor door that said NO ADMITTANCE. At the top the stairway the same key opened the door to the roof. In the A/C shack, Traci pulled out the foam pads she'd stored there. "Mind if I work on my seamless tan?" she asked.

"Who, me?" Stiles said. It was moot because Traci was already down to her toenail paint. A minute later, they were lying side by side, naked as jaybirds under a summer sky. The roof was a pretty setting, with the waving tops of eucalyptus trees filtering a view of the 101 curving south. Within half a mile stood the famous Capitol Records building, giving a Hollywood trope to the skyline.

Stiles poured from the thermos and they drank. "Thank God for creating gin," he said.

"Was that before or after he created man?"

"Probably before, first things being first."

She glanced at her wristwatch. "It's about time for the choppers from Downtown to come by. I can hear the beat."

Two LAPD helicopters soon appeared at two hundred feet, heading west. Traci came up on her knees and waved. She got a wave back. "I like to give those guys a cheap thrill," she said. "Captain McKnight will never hear about it, I guarantee."

"Here's to Uptight, the poor guy needs a break."

"Shall we ask him over?"

"Mm, not just now."

The sun was almost on the horizon and the gin was doing its work. The two detectives lay supine, just basking in the afterglow. It was so simple, so calming of the city's sonic dissonance.

Traci turned to look at him, taking her time. Tall, lithe, smooth of surface, not an ounce of fat anywhere to be seen. Shoulders that could slam an inked-up gangster, and arms that could hog tie him in 10 seconds. Legs bent now, his stomach flat, with his half empty glass balanced on it. His eyes were closed, his breathing slow and steady as a cat.

She thought back to the day they met. It was in Luttwak's corner office in the Hollywood station bull pen. Her request to be transferred to the Detectives table had been granted. When she entered the room, a terrific-looking guy in jeans and a blue track jacket was standing across from the lieutenant. She'd never seen him before.

Luttwak got to his feet. "Traci, I want you to meet Jack Stiles. Jack, this is Traci Little, the officer I was telling you about."

Stiles offered his hand. "Happy to meet you, Traci."

"Me too," was all she could come up with.

Luttwak went on. "Jack is one of our best detectives. I'm partnering you with him till you're comfortable with the drill. Now you two get outta here and share a desk."

That was the beginning of the most intuitive detective unit Hollywood ever had. Together they solved the messy murder of a socialite right off the bat. A lack of missing valuables ruled out burglary or home invasion. Insufficiency of physical evidence didn't help. The partners turned instead to the victim's personal relationships. Interviews with her friends and family members revealed some unexpected links. Mucking around those ultimately led to the person who had good reason to want her dead.

Not long after, Stiles asked Traci out for a drink.

"We're not supposed to be, um, involved," she said, giving him a smile that said otherwise.

"We can just talk about business."

"I don't want to talk about business. Do you?"

"No way. Write down your address, for me. I'll pick you up at seven."

That first date was a recognition that this would be no casual affair. It felt real, lasting, faithful, amazing. So forever.

Now, on the roof, watching him so innocently dozing, Traci was inspired to mischief. She leaned over to him and began a series of feathery kisses and watched him respond. The wine glass tipped and spilled. Her laughter was like a flute ascending the scale.

Meter maid Fran Lucas, a 12-year veteran of the Farmer's Market parking patrol, was issuing a citation in their 3rd and Fairfax lot when she remembered the BOLO. She radioed her supervisor and reported a Honda with tag no. 4STL2827. In a few minutes an undercover car responded with two plain clothes cops in it. They parked nearby waiting for Victor Krait to appear.

Krait, who sat two hundred feet away sipping on a latte, was too smart to be taken so easily. He knew for sure now that the Civic had to go.

Loss of the car was not a serious matter. He was tired of it anyway. He looked down at the black guitar case at his feet that contained the short barrel assault rifle. How fortunate that I didn't leave it in the trunk, he mused.

Krait took a slow and gassy bus ride to Calvin Scott's B of A branch at Sunset and Van Ness. In case the bank might be under surveillance, he waited across the street for his favorite teller to come out at lunch time. She was a 30-year-old brunette with almond eyes and a pretty smile. Her tag said Myrna Rainville, Assistant manager. She wore no ring.

Shortly after noon Myrna emerged, crossed the street and walked in his direction. He feigned surprise. "Oh, Miss Rainville, isn't it?"

"Why hello, Mr. Scott," she said. "I see you're starting a beard. I must say it fits you nicely."

"Just an experiment," Krait said. "How nice to run into you like this. I've been meaning to ask you about something."

"Any way I can help." There was the smile.

"How about lunch at the Italian place? We can talk. Unless you have other plans, of course."

"None that I can't cancel." In fact she had no plans and was thrilled to be asked. "That would be very nice. My name is Myrna, by the way."

"I know. I just didn't want to seem too forward. You may as well call me Calvin."

The place he had in mind was Di Paolo's, only half a block away. While they walked, he asked how her work was going.

"Pretty well. It's much the same thing every day," she said. "Actually, teller work is outright boring."

"Mm, what would you say if I asked you to be my personal banker?"

"I don't know. What would that entail?"

"Let's have a drink and we'll talk about it."

"All right, I'd love to."

They had reached Di Poalo's now. It was a pleasant place with seating along the sidewalk shaded by fig trees. A row of potted azaleas separated the diners from the foot traffic. A maroon-vested waiter took their drink order. Myrna chose white zinfandel and Krait did too, though it was too twee for him. When the wine arrived, he clinked his glass with hers. Again, her smile, and he decided this was the moment.

"All this has to do with an inherent phobia I have." He glanced away. "I'm embarrassed to even talk about it."

"No, please don't be."

"Well, you see, I get queasy inside the bank, where there's a lot of cash on hand and cameras on the wall and Federal rules posted everywhere on little cards. I know its just a silly little phobia, but that's the fact of it."

"I understand perfectly. Those overhead cameras are necessary, but do they really have to show the customers on-screen while they're standing in line? It only reminds them that there could be a robbery at any moment."

"Exactly. What I need is someone I can deal with right here in a softer ambiance. My transactions are large but few. We can have lunch like we're doing now, and do deposits and withdrawals in this pleasant setting. I would pay you a hundred dollars for every transaction."

"Oh, I couldn't do that. It's probably illegal anyway."

"Nonsense." Krait turned on the charm. He took her hand and said, "I have a confession, Myrna. I find you very attractive. I love your smile and your cheerfulness. I've noticed you're not wearing a ring. What a terrible waste of a lovely woman."

"Calvin, how sweet of you. Actually I see that you have no ring either. And yet you seem like someone who is deeply into life, someone who has a sense of romance."

"I know it's trite, my dear, but romance is what makes the world spin."

She raised her glass. "Here's to a little triteness now and then."

"Please allow me to take you to dinner tonight. We'll find a quiet place and discover everything about each other."

"But no hundred dollars."

"No, of course not. That would be cheap."

"Then let's do. We can have a nightcap at my place."

It was Victor Krait at his most propitious. There was a good chance he could change her mind about his "arrangement" to access his Zurich money without being rousted at the bank. And he'd found a new sex partner, he was certain. Not as beautiful as Carina, but very attractive nevertheless.

24

After day watch, The Full Clip was at its usual high resonance. The music system was blasting out a Tony Bennett big band recording from the nineties and some people were dancing on The Clip's dinky hardwood dance floor. At the bar Stiles ran into his friend Ted Redfern from the Rampart Division. He hadn't talked with him since the night Topo was arrested.

"Hey, Jack," Redfern hailed him. "You owe me a drink."

"I know. I've been trying to avoid you," Stiles said, giving him a fist bump.

Redfern ordered a Dos Equis, and they talked.

"I suppose you already know," Redfern said. "At the pre-lim Topo's shysters got him a postponement."

"They usually do, with Judge Pugmire. But on second request he always gets pissed off and denies any further motions. I hope I get to testify about Topo. I know more about that puke than his own mother does."

"Where's Traci tonight?"

"I don't know. Probably with her friend Kim. She's LAPD too, works at Records and Identification."

"I know her. A terrific looking girl." He didn't elaborate.

At this point, the two men were joined by Frank Roditi, Redfern's current partner.

"Hey, Frank," Stiles said, "Good to see you. You guys still working together?"

"Hey, Jack. I see you found my old buddy. We came up on Domestic Violence together."

"Ah, the table of broken dreams."

"How true. But now we're both working Homicide."

"I know," Stiles said. "Welcome to the nut house. Weird is always happening on that duty."

"Never a truer word," Roditi said and signaled for a beer. "Remember the 49th Street school shooting a few years back?"

"Yeah, I think so."

"That was when I was a rookie out of Hollenbeck before they moved. A sniper killed a 16-year-old girl just outside the schoolyard. Radio cars responded in minutes, cops all over the place. When we arrived, people on the sidewalk told us the shots had come from a house across the street. SWAT officers called to the scene fired several tear gas canisters into the house, but with no results. So the SWAT Commander ordered a forced entry."

"Oh, I remember that. The place where the door opens out instead of in, so nobody could use a battering ram."

"Right. The SWAT team pried off the entire frame in no time. Inside the door was a flight of stairs. They tossed a couple of flash-bang grenades up the stairs and rushed up there. They found the guy dead in his bedroom, a suicide. Searching the room they found a pump gun and an AR-15.

"So here's the kicker: It turned out that this was the same froot loop who for months had been shooting at planes landing at LAX."

"Coincidence is everything in cop work," Stiles said.

Redfern had a story. "A few years back, me and my first partner were on business downtown. We had lunch at a Chinese restaurant on Central Avenue. We were driving my personal car at the time. So after paying the tab we came out, and here parked in front was a Ford van with green stripes and no grille. Well, I remembered a few weeks before, a recycling place in the Valley got robbed by two suspects driving a green striped van with no grille. So we radioed the Ford's tag number.

"Two men came out and got into the van and drove away. We requested back up and began to follow. They must have seen us, but for some crazy reason these two morons turned into a gas station right up against a wall. We pulled up behind and blocked them. Minutes later two Patrol cars arrived and rousted them. The P/Os found a gun hidden under the dash. And these guys were out on bail at the time."

"There you go again. Pure coincidence."

At that moment, two men dressed in hoodies walked into the Full Clip and fired two pistol shots into the ceiling. The music cut off. Some people froze and others ducked for cover.

"This is a stickup!" the super-sized one shouted. "Everybody git down!" The other guy had filthy dreadlocks hanging out. Both were black, and apparently they had no clue they'd stumbled into a cop bar.

They wised up in a hurry when the two bartenders jacked the shotguns they stashed behind the well. Ten LAPD cops pulled out their carry guns and drew a bead on them. One was Dick Cheevers, a formidable black man himself.

"Drop yo weapons and kick 'em away," Cheevers ordered, adding a little flavor to it. "Hands on yo head, face away from me. Do it now!" There wasn't a whole lot else the stickup mopes could do. Two of the cops who were there searched them and cuffed them to a brass pole. Lieutenant Luttwak happened to be there that night. He used his cell to request a 2-man patrol unit to take the men away.

The music went back on and Tony Bennett took over.

Ted Redfern and Jack Stiles had been in the same class at the Academy. Stiles had gone on to Hollywood while Redfern ended up at Rampart, where he currently worked with Roditi.

Redfern wished he'd been able to stick with Stiles. Frank was a solid cop, but they had no special empathy. There wasn't a whole lot to talk about except cops and crime.

Roditi wasn't exactly an intellectual giant. His reading consisted of USA Today, People, and other rags commonly found in doctor's waiting rooms. Well that was all right, he had plenty of poker friends and fellow Dodger fans to fill his free time. Redfern's interests were wider, fed by a deep curiosity about the world around him. He was up to date in current news and politics, and read creative fiction whenever he had time. Too bad Rampart didn't afford him much time.

Both men were single. Roditi was a skirt chaser, which was okay with the sort of skirts he chased. Redfern's approach was thoughtful and selective. He would love to have a steady girlfriend, but so far he hadn't found anyone that intrigued him. Until Kim Kaelin, a girl he knew in Records and Identification, a Division he frequently contacted in his work.

Redfern had a serious crush on Kim. The problem was, she was so good-looking that he feared she was out of his league or already involved with someone. In truth, Kim was tired of being hit on by every loose guy on the block. She was looking for someone she could be serious about. Maybe that someone could be Ted.

She would flirt with him when he called the Records land line, but that of course was limited. So she gave him her personal cell number. From that point on they talked at night, and that's when things started to heat up.

"Hi, you," she said recognizing him.

"Want to talk?"

"Sure. Hold on a sec." A minute and she picked up again.

"That's better. I wanted to get more comfortable."

"You're in a long night gown and a frilly cap and carrying a candle, right?"

Her laugh was a little husky. "Uh, not exactly."

"I didn't think so. What, then?

"You absolutely sure you can handle it?"

"Try me."

"You asked for it. I'm wearing SWAT team body armor and gummy boots."

Redfern's turn to laugh. "You've been on duty too long."

"I know it. Records is monsterly boring. By the end of watch, my mind is absent of any useful thought."

"I don't blame you. Just be calm and relaxed and completely open."

"Okay, so I'm down to my skivvies."

"Really. What a coincidence."

"Yeah, too bad I never have phone sex before midnight."

"I can stay up for that."

In the moment now, Redfern got his nerve up. "What I really called about was to ask if you were free Saturday night."

"You mean for an actual date?"

"Yes."

"Just you and me, no paparazzi?"

"No way."

"Mm, I'll check my calendar, Teddybear."

That's what she called him after that.

25

Myrna Rainville was floating in a sea of euphoria. After dinner and flirty conversation and a bottle of Cotes du Rhone at her apartment, she was tingling. This charming man was actually undressing her. She helped him with her zipper and fell naked into his arms. As they kissed she could feel this hands caressing her bare bottom, and the world spun faster. This would be the opening act in a play of forbidden love.

In his seductive scheme Krait had portrayed himself as a successful commodity trader whose intuitive sense of timing had made him a rich man. He didn't mention that he'd done this while stealing other people's names. Myrna had no reason to doubt him. The transfers of large amounts from Zurich that she converted into cash for him fit his plans perfectly.

He told her that he wanted to pay in cash for a new car. Cash and his signature was always the way he did business, he said. Apparently that explanation was sufficient for her. At their next encounter, sure enough down the street to Di Poalo's she came with $30, 000 in U.S. banknotes in her tote. He signed the withdrawal slip for her, completing the transaction.

The following day, Krait purchased a new black Lexus coupe. Myrna accompanied him to the dealer's showroom and watched him hand over the currency to a dumbstruck auto salesman. The man had handled thousands of dollars in checks and credit card transactions in his day, but this was the first time he'd handled $30,000 in actual high denomination U.S. banknotes. Leery of counterfeit, he had the money cleared at a nearby bank. It was as real as money gets. With the deal signed and sealed, Krait threw his black case with the Bushmaster into the trunk and off they drove.

Meanwhile, Krait's old Honda sedan that security officer Fran Lucas had ticketed at the Farmers Market was examined by technicians at the LAPD Forensic Analysis Section. In the driver's compartment, traces of blood were discovered by the Serology/DNA unit. These matched blood samples of Carina Parra from the murder scene. Hair strands from the Honda matched those found at the Clyde Crawley crime scene. DNA from the hairs matched Victor Krait's samples from Terminal Island.

Luttwak and his detectives knew that Krait would be needing another car. A heads-up was issued to Los Angeles car dealers to be on the lookout for any vehicle purchase or test drive by Victor Krait aka Calvin A. Scott.

Another night, another murder in the heart of Hollywood.

In response to an urgent 911 domestic violence call, Radio Telephone Operator dispatched a 2-man patrol unit. Occupants at the address on Sunset Plaza did not respond to door knocks. A chilling scream was heard from inside the residence. The two P/Os secured a battering ram and broke the door in. They found a woman on the floor with a barbecue fork planted in her chest. A cursory examination showed that she was dead.

In the bedroom a man sat on the side of a double bed mumbling chapter and verse from the Bible. He was coherent but unresponsive. The Patrol unit in charge handcuffed the Bible man to the bed, called for backup, and began a search of the premises.

At 2015 hours, well after his watch had ended, detective Irv Miller received a call from lieutenant John Luttwak.

"Irv, there's been a murder at Sunset Plaza and Belfast Avenue. Round up Kaz and get over there."

"I know where that is. My daughter works in a boutique on Sunset."

"Good. If Kaz isn't available try Ed Chase. The Field Unit van is already over there."

"Who got killed?"

"A woman. There's also a man there muttering to himself. You'll see two black and whites in front. See officer Porcella."

"Okay, we'll take care of it."

By the time Miller and Kazurian arrived, three black and whites were in front. Several neighbors were standing in the street and the press had a late-hour crew on site. P/Os David Porcella and Hector Sanchez, who'd answered the 9-1-1 call, were taping off the entire area. Miller and Kazurian showed their Badge/ID wallets to Porcella.

"What have you got, man?" Irv said.

"One woman dead with multiple stab wounds, a lot of blood, and a man sitting on the bed ignoring us."

"Are they man and wife, do you know?"

"A couple of the neighbors say so. Mr. and Mrs. Konigsburger. They say the man hasn't been making much sense lately, like he's under too much stress."

"How about evidence?"

"Some broken stuff. A cell phone on the floor. Blood splatter on the wall, some on him."

"And the weapon?"

"A barbecue fork. No barbecue, though."

Kazurian said, "Let's take a look."

There wasn't much else to look at, really. A Field Unit crew was at work photographing the scene for splatter analysis, and gathering other materials for evidence. One tech was taking blood samples for his kit. It looked like typical domestic violence. Both the individuals were in their fifties at least.

"Maybe they just got sick of each other," Kaz said.

"More like he got sick of her," Irv said. "She doesn't look too appetizing."

"Let's talk to him." They found Konigsburger sitting on the bed with a King James bible open on his lap. He didn't acknowledge them with the slightest glance. Irv glanced over his shoulder and saw the book was open to Deuteronomy 32: 35, which he was muttering over and over—"To me belongeth vengeance and re-compense, for the day of their calamity is at hand and the things that shall come upon them—"

"Mr. Konigsburger, will you talk with us?" Irv said.

The man looked at them through rheumy eyes. "Are you from the Promised Land?"

"No, sir, we're from the police department."

"The police of Israel?"

"I'm afraid not. We're LAPD detectives and you are under arrest. Stand up and face the wall." Kazurian freed him from the bed and cuffed him again for transport. Miller bagged his bible for evidence. No way could they handle Konigsburger at Hollywood. They brought him to Headquarters downtown for booking.

Irv said, "What do you think, Kaz, is this for Homicide or Domestic Violence, or both?"

"I haven't the faintest," Kaz said. "Wak can wrestle with that one."

Around the detectives busy squad room, the murder became known as "the guy who forked his wife" case.

Myrna Rainville invited Krait into her life, her apartment and her bed. His seductive attentions transformed her into an entirely different woman. She changed her hairstyle and used more eye makeup. She bared her shoulders and shortened her skirt length by eight inches. Her legs were good and she knew it. At work she wore flats, with Krait she wore heels. Her movements became more relaxed, more fluid.

Myrna loved the black Lexus and the way Krait handled it, and her. He took her to restaurants and galleries, including a Hockney retrospective at MOMA. He seemed to have limitless money from Zurich to spend on her. And these breathless summer nights with him were a revelation of quirky sex.

One night on the way back from Disney Hall, he said to her, "I love that dress, the way the skirt slithers so nicely."

"Darling, that's why I chose it."

"Unlock your seat belt and come sit close to me."

"All right. How's this?"

"Perfect. Now take off your panties."

"Are you serious?"

"Don't be afraid, dear. Just put them in the glove box."

Her heart began racing, but she complied.

He slipped his hand between her legs. "Victor, this is crazy," she breathed, feeling the pulsations rising deep within her.

"Just lie back and enjoy," he said.

Before Victor, Myrna couldn't possibly have conceived of such a thing.

26

The accountant at the Lexus agency where Krait had paid in actual U. S. banknotes was having uneasy thoughts about the transaction. There was no problem depositing the money, but it almost felt like a Mafia deal. After debating the matter with himself, he decided to play it safe and inform the police. He called the Hollywood station and reported what he knew.

John Luttwak was definitely interested. Cheevers and Chase were next up, and he assigned them to check it out. The first thing Cheevers did was to call the agency and talk to the manager. He asked what the purchaser's name was. When the answer turned out to be Calvin A. Scott, the two detectives checked out a pool car.

At West Los Angeles Toyota, Cheevers and Chase met with Howard Bradley, the salesman who'd sold the vehicle.

"Thanks for seeing us, Mr. Bradley," Cheevers said.

"Call me Howie. We like it informal around here."

"Sure. This is my partner, Ed Chase."

"Hi, Ed. So how can I help the LAPD?"

"We're here about the guy you sold the Lexus coupe to, Calvin A. Scott. Could you describe him for us?"

Bradley could. "Tall, about fifty, looks a little like Jeremy Irons with a starter beard. We have a number of security cameras around. I'm sure we have him on tape."

"Good. We'll need that tape for evidentiary purposes."

"Was anyone with him at the time?" Chase asked.

"Yes, a young woman. A real looker, brunette, about thirty. Had a nice smile. I've seen her somewhere before but I can't think where."

"She come on like his daughter?"

Bradley laughed. "No way."

"Did the guy bring a trade-in car?" Cheevers asked.

"No, it was a straight cash deal. No checks involved, just U.S. fifties and hundreds all in a bunch. First time I've seen that, but it worked out okay."

"Besides the tape, we'll need copies of the transaction papers, vehicle model, color and specifications, Vehicle ID number, engine number—you get the drill."

"I'll run you a copy of the bill of sale. All that sort of info is on there."

"Thanks, the LAPD always appreciates a car dealer's help."

How true that was, the detectives knew.

Back at Hollywood Division, they reported their findings to Luttwak. The lieutenant in turn issued another All Points Bulletin: Be on the lookout for black Lexus coupe—license tag 7TMA4298, VIN 763607188. Suspect driver is Victor Krait aka Calvin A. Scott, wanted for homicide. Suspect may be heavily armed. Observe, but do not approach without backup. The "heavily armed" line was especially prescient. The fully loaded Bushmaster and a spare magazine lay ready in Krait's trunk.

Forcing all thoughts of Myrna from his mind, Krait turned to the impending destruction of Jack Stiles.

He thought back to his father's hatred of the evil forces of the law. The old man's admonition was simple: "Never hesitate to act. Make your plans and follow them to the finale. That's why I named you Victor. Above all, don't let yourself be distracted. If you do, you will fail." Krait had always followed that advice, and he'd been successful at every turn but one.

At a camera store, he found what he'd been looking for, a set of Steiner 8x30 military binoculars. These were noted for the brightness of their image. He could use them day or night in pursuit of his target.

Krait did not procrastinate. The very next day he began to surveil 1358 North Wilcox Avenue, the location of the LAPD Hollywood Division. He found a parking space a block down Wilcox on the other side of the street, near S-O-S BAIL BONDS. Next door to the S-O-S office was a gated garage where black and white patrol cars were being serviced.

Unconcerned, Krait began to observe the station's front elevation. The building had been completely redone in 2002, long since Krait's early days in Los Angeles. In place of the gloomy old masonry pile it once was, the building now had a pleasant red brick facade shaded by a row of ficus trees along the sidewalk. The entrance was a 15-foot recess in the brick with a few steps up to glass doors. The building's only identification was a vertical lighted sign saying POLICE.

At this early hour there was very little foot traffic on the street. He noticed a hooker in a Raider's jacket, shorts, and black mesh stockings pass by the door without causing the slightest stir. Gradually a few people began to arrive—complainants, office personnel, detectives, lawyers, witnesses and later on, some Asian visitors on a tour. It was hard to tell exactly who was what.

A secured parking lot was located just south of the building. It was filled with black and white patrol cars. To the right of the entrance a red octagonal sign said:

> STOP!
> NO PUBLIC PARKING
> POLICE VEHICLES ONLY

Seeing a number of sedans and sport utilities lined up along the side of the building, Krait correctly deduced that this was where cops parked their personal vehicles. Toward the back of the lot, he saw patrol cars checking in and leaving again with different personnel. Twice he saw handcuffed suspects being taken into the building.

At noon a few staffers came out to the parking lot and drove off to lunch. It struck Krait how lax and self-evident the whole operation seemed to be. Didn't they ever wonder who might be watching them come and go from their stupid building?

Tomorrow he would be back again, certain that he would learn which of the personal vehicles belonged to Jack Stiles. A day later he knew it was the red Mustang.

After 12 hours on an inter-agency narcotics operation, Stiles felt an urgent need to be with his partner, and not anywhere near Rampart's crowded gang-ridden streets. He started the Mustang and drove out of the Hollywood parking lot heading for Sunset and then west toward Traci's condo. She had logged out earlier, he knew.

According to his normal practice, Stiles would have checked his mirrors to see who was behind him, but not tonight. He was imagining Traci, what she might be doing right now. Taking a shower? Brushing her hair? Sorting her mail? He was not aware of the black Lexus coupe on his tail.

Victor Krait followed Stiles' mustang to a 3-story residential building in West Hollywood and watched it pull into the gated parking level. Krait parked nearby on the street. He retrieved the Bushmaster from his trunk, along with a spare magazine. He found a comfortable spot behind a privet hedge near the exit. The exit itself was fairly well lit. When the gate slid aside and Stiles drove out, Krait would blow him away. In his mind he saw the burst of fire ripping the detective to bloody shreds.

Stiles parked and took the elevator to the third floor. Traci answered his knock in shorts and a T-shirt, barefoot, looking like a college girl. She pulled him inside and slipped her arms around him.

"Missed you today," she breathed.

"Me too, but I didn't have time to call you."

"Mean streets, huh."

"Yeah, too busy bracing dealers and their runny-nosed clients. There's just no end to it." He removed his gear and service weapon and placed them on the side board.

"Poor baby. What you need is a drink."

"That would be nice," he said, and plopped down on the sofa. "I also need you and me in a normal setting, acting like real people."

"We're real enough, dear. It's the City that's cockeyed."

"It's full of thugs, that I know. Those fuckers are like leaky plumbing. You shut'em down in one place and they squirt out in another."

"Hm, you're worse off than I thought."

Traci went to her mini-bar and uncorked a bottle of Napa chardonnay, and poured two glassfuls. Returning, she knelt next to him, juggling the two glasses. "Try this, detective," she said.

"Here's to you, sweetheart," he said, channeling Bogart.

"Ah, so you're alive after all. Would you like me to warm up some lasagna?"

"Thanks, but I had a bite at four o'clock."

"Me too, actually."

Stiles drank deeply from the glass. "You know, I keep thinking of that drive we took up to the Channel Islands and what fun it was, and how it lifted our spirits."

"Yeah, that was sweet."

"I loved the sight of you sitting there in your silver bikini with your hair flying wild.

Traci laughed. "It's the Mustang's fault."

Stiles pulled her close just to breathe her scent.

"Don't spill," she said.

On the street below, Krait realized that Stiles wouldn't be coming out. No problem, he mused, he would simply wait until morning. Indeed, daylight would better serve his purpose.

27

The City at night, its powerful throb now a low murmur. Office buildings and apartment towers still glittering, traffic on freeways and boulevards still snaking along in streaks of red light. 9,862,049 citizens sleeping, plus those who hid from the census. Thousands of zygotes waiting to breathe. 50 years after the pill, hundreds of unexpected pregnancies still in the making. In late-night restaurants and bars, Studio big shots negotiating for properties that lack even a title.

The LAPD was out there, as always. Black and white patrol cars cruising gang-ridden neighborhoods trying to look like twice that many. John Luttwak's detectives hoping for once their cells wouldn't ring. Stiles and Traci in her queen-size bed with her head on his shoulder, breathing deep.

At five AM a timer clicked, and played "Strangers in the Night." Stiles got up and headed for the shower. In a few minutes he was dry and wide awake. Traci was still asleep with the sheet at half mast, looking glorious. Give her a few minutes, Stiles thought, and went to the kitchen to start the coffee maker. He dressed and strapped on his belt with his holstered Baretta on his right hip, his cell phone in the left, and handcuffs and badge behind. He slipped into his nylon track jacket with two spare magazines in the left pocket. He kissed his sleepy partner and left.

The elevator opened at the parking level and Stiles walked to his car. This time he observed the area through the open concrete columns. He noticed a black Lexus parked sixty meters up the street. Probably nothing, he thought, but he took no chances. He popped the trunk, pulled out his shotgun and a bag of shells and placed them on the seat beside him. He loaded four in the magazine and chambered one.

Krait watched Stiles' Mustang approach the exit bar. It was now or never. He shouldered his SBR, eye to the optics, and squeezed off three rapid shots. Two slugs slammed into the Mustang's door. Stiles bailed out of the passenger side and the car shuddered to a stop. He grabbed the shotgun and scrambled for cover behind the engine block. His left side at the belt line hurt like hell, and he knew he'd been hit. Blood ran down his leg. He took off his T-shirt and held it against the wound.

Upstairs, Traci heard the Bushmaster's unmistakable bam-bam-bam. She looked out the window and saw Krait hunched in the bushes. He fired five more rounds. That made eight. She whipped into her shorts and fleece top, grabbed her Glock and and hurried down the back stairs. She exited the back door and ran into the garden area.

Moving carefully, Traci flanked Krait's position and set up behind a pillar. Krait fired several more shots and she counted to twenty. There was silence. Traci knew Bushmasters had 20- and 30-round magazines. It meant Krait was changing clips.

Traci moved closer and raised her weapon. "LAPD!" she shouted. "Drop your gun and get your hands where I can see them!" Krait wasn't going to do any dropping and raising. He swung the SBR around. It was a fatal mistake. Stiles came up into his stance and fired the shotgun, jacked another shell and fired again. He shot Krait to death, in fact killed him twice. First by blowing away most of his skull and then by destroying his gut on the way down. The once-handsome triple murderer was reduced to a heap of bloody tissue ready for the Coroner.

Traci hurried to Stiles to make sure he was all right. She was shocked to see his T-shirt pad leaking red. "My God, you're shot," she said.

"I'm all right, partner," he sighed. "Thanks for backing me up."

Traci used the Rover in the Mustang to report shots fired, officer down, suspect dead, ambulance requested, code 3. In minutes Traci heard its siren. Three patrol units were dispatched to provide assistance and secure the area.

Soon the shooting scene was swarming with Field Unit personnel. Interviews were conducted for the crime log. Stiles was rushed to Hollywood Presbyterian to be treated. Two hours later the Coroner's van arrived to take custody of Krait's body.

Jack's through-and-through wound was painful but not serious. Emergency Room medics cleaned it out with antibacterial solution and injected him with amoxicillin, and gave him a bottle of amoxi caplets to take home. They also offered him two oxycodone pills, one of which he gave back.

Cheevers and Chase came to his bedside at Hollywood Pres to talk to him and wish him well.

"So you okay, man?" Cheevers said to him.

"Yeah. My body is made out of kevlar, you know that."

"Hey, that's better than chocolate pudding."

"How did this happen?" Kaz asked. "Krait was always a step ahead of us and then all of a sudden, BOOM!"

"Traci and I were taking care of business and Krait showed up uninvited."

"How did he know?"

"Apparently he'd been following me for two or three days."

"Pretty easy to spot that Mustang."

"Maybe so, but I'd never let some putz get in the way of a great car."

"A few inches southeast," Miller said, "and you'd be singin' soprano the rest of your days."

"Please, you're making me nervous."

"Is there anything more we ought to know?" Kaz said.

"Nothing I can think of. Traci will be here later to pick me up."

"Traci's going to be taking care of you? Cool, man."

"It's only for transport."

"Don't believe it," Kaz said. "That girl will be looking after your ass one way or another."

John Luttwak would be there for him too. He made it a point to visit Stiles at Hollywood Pres the minute he could break free. That was late morning the next day. In the labyrinth that a big city hospital inevitably must be, he found him sitting up in bed in a two-patient room looking grumpy.

"So you finally stopped a bullet," Luttwak greeted him.

"Doesn't everybody?" Stiles said.

"I'm surprised it hasn't happened earlier, all the stuff you get into."

"Just like any cop, lieutenant. You know that."

"Well you got that psychopath Krait, and saved the LAPD a lot of sweat, and the taxpayers a lot of money."

"Spoken like a man who came up from the ranks."

Luttwak laughed. "That's true enough."

"Can you get me out of here? I feel like a prisoner in my own city."

"Tomorrow. You know what hospitals are like. They want to make sure there's no infection and no law suit."

"I suppose. So what's with Traci?"

"She's stuck at work. I've paired her with Cheevers until you are fit for duty again."

"Good. She likes Dick and trusts him."

Luttwak was looking ahead. "McKnight will probably fuss about why you were at Traci's place. But don't worry about it. I'll handle him."

"Thanks, boss. From one cop to another."

Luttwak looked at his watch. "I can't stay, Jack. The crooks of America are running loose. I want you back as soon as you can make it, and I want you back with Traci."

"How about this afternoon?"

"Maybe tomorrow. Get some sleep, Jack. Back at Hollywood you're going to need it."

28

Several people were affected directly by Krait's death.

The good-old-boy owner of Sammy's Guns and Ammo had a momentary chill. He'd followed ATF's regulations, but you never knew what the Feds could think up. Clyde Crawley's Arizona family members felt grateful for a vengeful providence. Clyde was a crook, they knew, but a granddaddy kind of a crook. And this monster had Krait killed him for no reason.

When Myrna Rainville turned on the evening news, she was shocked to the core. Police officers had killed a suspect named Calvin A. Scott in a shootout. The shocker was, Scott turned out to be someone else, Victor Krait, a triple murderer. To think this killer had explored every square inch of her, and she was loving it. He'd given her orgasms to die for. Merciful God, she could be dead right now.

Krait's Bushmaster was traced to Sevic Sorbo. Long under suspicion of trafficking in illegal firearms, Sorbo was arrested by Federal agents.

John Luttwak felt a great weight lifted from him. Lately he'd begun to wonder if Krait would ever be caught, much less shot. Then, out of nowhere, Jack Stiles killed him in the parking level of Traci Little's condo building. The two of them probably were upstairs in her bed moments before. There would be an inquiry, he knew that. He would do his best to thwart it. He needed Stiles and Traci to remain on his Homicide squad. And working together.

Liz was stunned when she heard that Traci had been involved in a shoot-out that killed one of the most wanted criminals in the City, and that LAPD officer Jack Stiles had been wounded in the exchange of fire. Jack, the detective with the red Mustang they were going to grace with a bikini crawl. The guy that Traci loved.

Suddenly their mission had taken on a new level of importance. Now the girls would be performing with greater energy and daring. That was fine with Liz. She had no qualms about it and neither would Traci and Kim.

In accordance with LAPD Rules and Procedures, Jack Stiles received 30 days paid leave because of injury. During his off time, he endured a couple of gassy sessions with the Shooting Review Board. In addition, forensic psychologist Diane Metz was asked to make sure he wasn't mentally affected.

She interviewed him in her office at the Behavioral Sciences Division downtown. It was far more pleasant than the spartan offices at Hollywood station. It had a window on the east side of the new LAPD Headquarters, with mini-blinds filtering a fine view of City Hall across 1st Street. Furnishings were comfortable, but absent of any style or color that could possibly skew her results.

"Thanks for coming, Jack. Please ignore all the manuals and psychology stuff."

"No ink blots?" Stiles said.

She laughed. "No blots. Let's sit in these comfortable chairs. I just need to make sure you're okay."

"No problem with that."

Diane turned on a tape machine and recited, "0800 hours 09/08/2011 at Hollywood Station. Interview with Homicide detective Jack Stiles, regarding officer-involved shooting death of suspect Victor Krait.

"Let's make it fast and clean, detective. What brought about the confrontation with the suspect?"

"Victor Krait's non-stop campaign to kill me."

"How do you know that?"

"Everybody at Hollywood knew it. But if you need chapter and verse, there's always Carina Parra's sworn statement."

"I'll settle for your version."

"The statement notes that I killed Krait's partner, Raphael Parra. But much more important to Krait was that I ruined his attempted bank robbery. My partner, Detective Little, arrested him fleeing the scene. He pled to a deal and served a dime at Terminal Island."

"And after he was released?"

"He proceeded to commit a series of crimes, starting with two brutal brutal murders. In the course of that he changed his identity twice. He wanted to disappear, so that he could carry out his plans."

"When did you become aware of this?"

"When he hired a friend of Parra's widow to plant a bomb in my car. The idiot blew himself up with it. You remember that. We suspected Krait was behind it and tried everything we knew to run him down. This wasn't easy because Krait was very clever. He kept changing names and changing cars. And he murdered Carina Parra along the way."

"All of that must have been frustrating for you."

"Very frustrating. The man was a stone killer on the loose, and we couldn't find him."

"Let's cut to the chase. How did you feel when you finally shot him?"

"I felt good. He deserved what he got."

"Who fired first?"

"Krait did. He was lying in wait for me."

"Did you shoot to kill?"

"Damn right. At that moment he was firing a short barrel assault weapon at me, 20 rounds in all. Thank God my partner Traci Little showed up and diverted his attention. I was able to use my pump gun and I didn't miss. Otherwise I wouldn't be sitting here talking to you."

"Any post-shooting mental trauma? Depression? Nerves? Nightmares?"

"Nothing. I killed him, no regrets."

"Anything else I need to know about?"

"Yeah, that son of a bitch shot holes in my Mustang."

"Thank you, detective. End of interview." Diane turned off the machine.

"You're okay, Jack."

"I have a feeling you knew that to begin with, Diane."

She had to laugh. "You're as sane as anyone I know."

Stiles took advantage of the thirty days leave to get his Mustang restored. Not get a new one, no way. This was the Mustang that had actually saved his life. LAPD Field Unit techs determined that the car had sustained 17 .223 caliber hits. The other rounds fired from Krait's magazine were found buried in concrete pilasters of the parking level.

Since the LAPD's insurance program only covers accidents and damage to official vehicles, Stiles was stuck with his own restoration costs. If he had been on duty at the time he could've filed a claim, but of course that was not the case. At least the Department could refer him to specialists skilled in repairing ordnance-damaged vehicles.

One fortunate thing was that the V-8 engine block had withstood SBR fire without damage. Bullet holes in the car's coachwork would have to be filled. Some of the upholstery would have to be redone and new tires would be needed. Finally the Mustang would repainted in the same sassy red.

The Full Clip was alive when Stiles walked in. He eased himself onto a bar stool next to Traci and ordered a Sam Adams. A few cops he knew came by to give him a high five. Immediately he began to feel better.

One of the P/Os extended his hand. "You're Jack Stiles, right?"

"Right. This is my partner, Traci Little."

"Happy to meet you, Traci. I'm Rick Onofre. You guys may remember me from catching the Clyde Crawley case."

"Oh yeah. We read your IR at the time."

"Too bad the old guy got blasted. He never gave us any trouble, you know. Thanks for putting down his killer. It's amazing the way weirdos like him keep coming out of the woodwork."

"I think it's mutation," Traci said. "Sometime along the line, radiation or a virus or God knows what happens, and you have some wild DNA on your hands."

"Not that it matters," Stiles said. "We have to deal with them."

"Right, and that means steady employment for cops."

"Here's to cops."

They raised their glasses. "Here's to cops!"

"And their little genes and chromos." Traci said.

Dick Cheevers was up to his usual ceremonial shtick. He rose and clinked on his glass.

"Ladies and gentleman, may I have your attention please. Let's give a big welcome to the renowned, the skilled, the totally irresponsible Jack Stiles!" Applause and cheers broke out for a full laid-back L.A. minute.

"As most of you know, Jack managed to blow away one of our City's most wanted criminals, identity thief and triple killer Victor Krait." Boos and hoots followed.

"This is truly amazing, since in all his fabled career, Jack never so much as broke a fingernail." Raucous laughter. "Hey, claws can be a real weapon in a snit!"

"But I digress. Now as to the real hero in this tale, detective Traci Little, we can thank her for wiggling her ass and yelling LAPD! As you know, this can be very distracting."

Traci couldn't resist. She was wearing a date dress and heels that night. She slid off her stool and aced a couple of salsa moves, setting off a chorus of whistles and woo-hoos.

"Thank you, Madam Lazonga." Cheevers went on. "Now this brings us to Jack's Mustang. That's a car that hot girls leap into like fish goin' upstream. It also has an engine block that sheds 9mm slugs like dandruff. Too bad Jack left his butt hangin' out."

"Up yours, Cheevers," Stiles said.

"You talkin' to me?" said Cheevers, a la De Niro.

"Seriously, though. Jack's car suffered a lot of hits and the repairs will cost a ton of money. But the LAPD policy doesn't cover cops' personal vehicles. So if you want to help, toss a few bucks into the Mustang pail on the bar." This was a complete surprise to Stiles. A small thing, perhaps, but touching.

Still, $554 and two lottery tickets ended up in the bucket that night.

29

By the time his car was fully restored, Stiles' wound no longer throbbed as it did in the early days of his recovery. The bandage was half the size of the original pad-and-tape job. If he bumped into something it hurt, though, and the world seemed full of door knobs.

He called Traci on her cell at work and she knew it would be him.

"Hi, partner," she said. "You okay?"

"Not bad. How about you?"

"I'm okay. They've got me paired with Dick for a while. He's fun to work with."

"A damn good cop too. You can trust him to back you up."

"I know. So, did you get your Mustang back?"

"I did, and it's beautiful. Even better than before."

"Terrific. You know, I can't talk from here just now." That was Traci's code for "I want to see you tonight."

"Sorry, I know you're busy," he said.

Traci answered the door in a terry towel, fresh from the shower and still damp. She slid her arms around his neck and held on like he might evaporate.

"God, it's been empty around here with you shot up and missing in action," she breathed.

"Sorry about that. Thanks for saving my ass by the way."

"My pleasure, dear. And how is your wound feeling now?"

"It's a little sore, but that'll go away eventually."

"Want some chardonnay?"

"I'm not suppose to have any, but yes."

"Okay. Relax while I uncork some Napa coastal." And she trotted away.

He plopped onto the sofa, grateful of its decadent comfort. He glanced around Traci's sunny condo. This is where I really belong, he mused, not in that scabby flat where I sleep. It's time I started the rest of my life. Why the hell not?

He heard fridge noises and a pop. Traci returned with a bottle, two wine glasses. She knelt close to him on the sofa and they drank like thirsty desert rats.

"Diane interviewed me," he said. "She asked me how I felt about shooting Krait. I told her I enjoyed it. I wanted to see him dead and I shot to kill. No regrets, except that I can't do it over again."

"Me too. I wept when I saw the blood soaking your leg."

"I wept when I saw all those holes in my Mustang."

"Out of anger?"

"No, out of gratitude."

They drank, sharing a few oaky, peachy, and apple-tinged kisses.

"What about sex?" Traci said. "Is that off the menu too?"

"The question never came up."

Stiles drained his glass. "Can I sleep with you tonight?"

"Silly question."

"I just want to be in bed with you. I want to run my hands all over you and tell you how much I love you."

"Wow." This was sweet as clover after a rain.

Captain McKnight wanted to know why detective Stiles had a key to the parking level below detective Little's condominium. He sent one of his inflated memorandums to John Luttwak demanding an explanation. Luttwak ignored him. Days later, McKnight descended to Luttwak's bullpen office.

"John, didn't you get my memo?"

"Yes, I did. Speaking plainly, I didn't agree with it."

"It's prima fascia. Stiles and Little are seeing each other. Don't you see that—"

Luttwak was busy with a Crime Report. His temper had been working up to this sort of confrontation for months.

"Captain, I have a Homicide squad to run, not a Hollywood gossip mill. I don't have time for this."

McKnight was indignant. "Lieutenant, when I address you I expect your full respect."

"Tell me something important and you'll get it."

"This is a serious matter. Detectives Stiles and Little are personally involved. That is unacceptable under Article VII of the Operational Rules and Procedures—"

Luttwak got up from his chair. "Captain, I've tried to be accommodating, but frankly I've had it with you and your memos. Just keep your fingerprints off my Homicide detectives. We're too busy to put up with your nonsense."

"This is insubordination. Apologize, or I will file a complaint with the BOPC."

Luttwak was plain angry. "Go ahead. The Commissioners are competent and they know what police work is about. My reply will be that you are well past it, and should be retired to a golf condo in Limp Dick, Arizona."

"You haven't heard the last of this, Lieutenant." McKnight huffed. Both men knew it was an empty threat. Any level of PC inquiry would reveal McKnight's total incompetence.

The trial of Sevic Sorbo took place at the Federal Building in downtown Los Angeles in the walnut paneled courtroom of U.S. District

Judge Charles Morganstern. At the defense table, Sorbo's attorneys presented him in a tailored suit, white shirt and striped tie. But there was no way to disguise the dark glower on his Slavic face.

After two weeks of voir dire, a jury and three alternates were installed and the trial began. Morganstern, noted for his intolerance of pointless blather, moved the proceedings forward with all deliberate speed.

In concert with ATF, the LAPD had been investigating Sorbo for weeks. The scope of the inquiry and the quality of its witnesses were damning. The resulting testimonial brick wall erected by ADA James Presley, and the feeble attempts of defense attorneys to poke holes in it, left the jurors with little to debate. They wasted no time in finding Sorbo guilty of illegal arms trafficking and accessory to murder. Appeals were speedily denied. Six weeks later sentencing was rendered.

Judge Morganstern ordered the defendant to rise.

"Mr. Sorbo, before I determine your sentence, I ask you if you have anything to say."

Sorbo had nothing to say. He simply spit on the floor.

"The record shall indicate no verbal reply. So let us now proceed. Mr. Sorbo, a jury of your peers has found you guilty of the charges brought against you in this court of law. You have been ably represented by attorneys provided you, and you have been shown every consideration of fairness by the court. Hearing no apology, no words of remorse, I now must see that justice is done.

"I won't mince words, Mr. Sorbo. You are no big deal. You are nothing but a pustule on the face of decent society. For the misery and death you have caused to innocent men, women and children in the pursuit of your criminal agenda, I hereby sentence you to 30 years of penal confinement in San Quentin State Prison at San Rafael, California. Parole eligible after 80 percent of time served."

Morganstern banged his gavel and ordered, "Bailiff, take him away." He gathered his robes and exited to chambers with no further comment.

22: 30 hours. This Hollywood murder was one of the bloodiest Cheevers could remember—blood on the carpet, spatters on the wall, drag marks. A woman's body was soaked in it. This would be a challenge for LAPD forensics personnel.

"I hate stabbings," Cheevers said. "What a godforsaken mess." He kept clear of the Field Unit that was photographing the scene and logging various samples into evidence bags. A silver carving knife still lay on the floor.

"Why do they kill the pretty ones?" Traci said.

"Shit, I don't know. Some people are born sick, I guess."

"I wonder who gave birth to this one."

"We'll find out before it's over," Cheevers said.

Traci observed the body without getting in the way. "She didn't go down without a fight. Look at her fingernails. There's DNA in there for sure."

One of the P/Os came over. "The husband is in the den. Says he came home and found her like this. He's major broke up over it."

"We need to interview him." Cheevers said. Not exactly my favorite duty."

"Copy that, partner."

They found Matt Corbyn sitting on an Italian off-white leather sofa with his head in his hands. In fact all the seating was imported. At one end, a 42-inch TV was showing a Laker game with the sound off. Watercolors of golf scenes were on two of the walls, and a bookcase with trophies against another. A bar with liquor bottles and glasses stood in one corner, waiting. This was upper middle class all the way.

"I'm detective Cheevers, LAPD, and this is detective Little." They showed their ID/ badge wallets. "We're sorry about this, Mr. Corbyn," Traci said.

Corbyn looked up at the two cops. "Thank you. Now get the son of bitch who did this to Fauna."

"Don't worry, we will," Cheevers said. "But we'll need your total cooperation."

"I know it. I'm just falling apart. Nothing in my life ever prepared me for discovering this horrible scene."

"We understand," Traci said. "We're designating you as a victim here. However you're also a person of interest."

"Listen, I want to state categorically that I didn't kill Fauna. I'm a peaceful man, incapable of killing a mouse."

"Duly noted," Cheevers replied. He indicated the Field Unit working the crime scene. "In a day or two we should have more information, and we may want to talk to you again. Where can you be reached?"

"Here's my cell phone number. You can reach me there at any time."

"Thank you. Before you go I need to swab you for DNA."

"Absolutely no objection," Corbyn said.

30

September was the last of the really warm months. Even in Southern California there came a time of reckoning with the gods of fall. The first Saturday of the month was a blend of clear skies, rosy afternoon sunlight and gentle air, and a confluence of time-off schedules. Perfect for the Mustang shoot.

Jack Stiles drove his resurrected car onto a chained and padlocked service road in upper Griffith Park. The entry was courtesy of Ted Redfern, who used to brace pot smokers up there and still had a key. Aboard were Ted and three of Hollywood's most high-spirited females—Traci, Liz, and Kim Kaelin. Two were in bikinis. Kim wore white shorts and a knotted shirt with nothing under. All were up for a free and breezy afternoon. Stiles had brought along a couple of gallon-size containers in a cooler, one filled with martinis and the other with margaritas. Nobody really cared which.

The eponymous Mustang photo party was an excuse to run loose and show a lot of skin. It began innocuously enough with much leaping and laughing and chasing Kim's Frisbee and drinking God knows how much booze. On the nearby meadow, Redfern was keeping the girls on the fly. Stiles sat on the cooler nursing a martini, watching it all happen.

Twenty hyperventilating minutes later, Traci called Liz and Kim into a huddle.

"It's time to get our show on the road," she panted. "Jack's really been through it, getting hit in the shoot-out with that lunatic Victor Krait."

"Plus that petrifying 30-day medical leave."

"Right. So let's treat him to a totally dynamite Mustang crawl."

"How can we miss?" Liz said. "We're ninety-five percent bare just standing here."

Traci laughed. "I'm aware of it. But the main thing is the mood. Let's keep it frothy and fun."

"Definitely frothy and fun," Liz echoed.

"Especially frothy." Kim said, and the huddle broke up.

"What was all that about?" Stiles wanted to know.

"Three hot girls getting set to crawl all over your car." Traci said. "And you get to shoot it."

Liz gave the Nikon to Stiles. "This is an SLR, you see exactly what the lens sees. Rotate this to zoom in and out."

"Got it," Stiles said. He looped the strap around his neck.

Kim led off, sitting in the cockpit with the door open and one leg still on the turf, a classic view of a streaky-blond American girl in a legendary American car. Redfern loved it. Stiles nailed it, and the session took off from there.

Traci followed. She mounted the Mustang's hood in her silver space girl triangles, thrusting herself forward like an Art Deco radiator cap from a 1930s cabriolet. Stiles shot it a dozen ways. Liz decided to turn up the heat. She deployed on the rear deck with her breasts masked by her fingers, as might be seen on a Sports Illustrated swimsuit cover. Stiles had always wondered how Traci's sister would look naked. Now he mostly knew, and he wasn't disappointed.

Any part of a Mustang that could support a girl's body served as a backdrop—windshield, head rests, rear seats with legs flung to the sky. Yards of apricot-tinted skin against chrome and shiny red paint. Stiles caught it all.

Kim Kaelin came to him. "Can I have the camera, Jack?"

"Sure. Got something in mind?"

"Uh huh. Teddy needs a little encouragement. I'm going all out to supply him with it."

She brought the Nikon over to Redfern. "Take my picture, Teddy?"

"I'd love to." He strapped it around his neck.

"Where do you want me?"

"How about against the driver's door?"

"Okay." Kim planted her butt on the door sill with her legs straight out. Settled and at ease, she untied her shirt and tossed it away. "How's this?" she said.

Redfern didn't see it coming. "Wow" was all he could say. Through the lens, he could see Kim smiling at him with her arms crossed under her breasts, looking terrific. Never mind the car, he zoomed in on Kim, framing her from the waist up.

"Just tell me what you'd like," she said.

"I like you just as you are." He clicked three shots.

"Chin down a teeny bit."

"Like this?"

"Yeah." He clicked three times more, and said, "Change it a little."

She shook out her hair and gave him a look. Click, click.

Jack and Traci and Liz stood by, utterly transfixed. Apparently Redfern had a latent twist of creativity lurking somewhere in his DNA.

"Shoulders up a little, sweetheart." Click, click, click.

"Give me a big smile and a wiggle," he said. And she did, laughing.

"Super. Change it again." Click, click.

"Straighter, prouder." Click, click, click, click, click.

"Perfect." Click, click, click. "That's a wrap."

Kim hurried to him and threw her arms around his neck.

"Thank you, Teddybear," she breathed in his ear. "That was so fun."

"I loved you," he said, not wanting to let her go. Both were oblivious of the applause.

Luttwak summoned his Corbyn homicide investigators to his partitioned office. It was friendlier than the interview room, mainly due to its window. Drawing up chairs were Dick Cheevers, Traci Little and Jack Stiles, still on leave but there nevertheless. Luttwak offered doughnuts and coffee with creamer and little wooden sticks to stir with. All but Stiles had laptops, notepads and 9"x12" blue file folders containing a preliminary report of the Fauna Corbyn case.

Luttwak wasted no time. "So what's new that we know?"

Cheevers turned on a recorder. "This is a tape of yesterday's interview with Matt Corbyn. The voice you may not recognize is Corbin's attorney, Miles Igbal. You may hear ADA Jim Pressley on there too."

The tape rolled. First, the sound of Igbal unsnapping his briefcase, then saying, "We've been through that before, detective, so let's move on."

Cheever's voice: "All right. Mr. Corbyn, were relations between you and your wife amicable?"

Matt Corbyn: "Generally, yes. That was before we drifted apart and were talking about divorce."

Cheevers: "Did you have any indication that she might be seeing someone else?"

Corbyn: "Yes, I knew it from her computer log." Sigh. "I guess all this makes me suspect number one."

Cheevers: "Not necessarily. Now, do you know the name of the person your wife was seeing?"

Corbyn: "Yes. James Ripinski."

Cheevers: "How do you know that?"

Corbyn: "I followed them. I found out where he lives. I also found out they were sucking our savings accounts dry."

Cheevers: "Is that why you killed her?"

Sound of Igbal rapping his pen on the table. "You don't have to answer that. You've already strongly denied killing her."

Traci: "So what did they do with the money?"

Corbyn: "Fauna transferred it to a different bank in a joint account with Ripinski."

Traci: "When you discovered that what did you do?"

Corbyn: "I cashed in our remaining savings certificates."

Traci: "I meant regarding your wife."

Corbyn: "There was a big fight. I called her a cheating bitch. She threw a silver teapot at me. A wedding present, would you believe."

Cheevers: "And you grabbed another wedding present and stabbed her to death."

Sound of Igbal scraping his chair. "This interview is over. Let's go, Matthew."

Pressley: "Not so fast, attorney. Where can we find James Ripinski?"

Corbyn: "He lives in Sherman Oaks."

End of tape.

"Interesting," Luttwak said. "I'm beginning to believe the guy."

"Me too," Cheevers said.

"What about the Coroner's report?"

"Nineteen stab wounds," Traci said. "The first two or three could've killed her."

"Son of a bitch ought to be hung from a lamppost," Stiles commented. "I'll hold the rope."

"What about trace evidence?"

"DNA was recovered from her nails, but no match from the FBI CODIS data base as yet."

"Okay. Good job, Dick," Luttwak said. "At this point, I'm switching back to our normal format. Seeing as Jack is fit now I'm pairing him with Traci again, and you'll be back in your regular slot with Ed Chase."

"Anything you want, boss," Cheevers said.

Luttwak turned to Stiles and Traci. "You two pick up James Ripinski. See if he has any scratches."

Normally oblivious Jack Stiles found the good grace to thank Traci, Liz and Kim for the sexy treat they had given him. From the Nikon's memory card, he chose the best of the Mustang shots and sent a set of professionally done 11x14 prints to each of them. An accompanying note said,

> *Dear Mustang Girls,*
> *Thanks for the wonderful bikini tease you performed all over my car. There's nothing like bare female skin to raise a guy's spirits in these chancy times.*
> *I'm returning the camera to you, Liz. Don't worry about the pictures ending up on-line. I deleted them and trashed the memory card.*
> *Jack*

31

Not only did James Ripinski have no scratches, but neither did Matt Corbyn. Further, their DNA didn't match the DNA recovered from Fauna Corbyn's fingernails. This left the investigators with no suspect and no leads.

Time for Plan B to trot in from the bullpen. A search was made for DNA profiles similar to those at the crime scene. A California Justice Department criminal data base produced a list of 170 such profiles. These were further tested for the Y chromosome present in male familial relationships. A single profile emerged—that of Melvin Ripinski who was currently serving time for grand theft auto. Obviously he couldn't have been Fauna Corbyn's slayer. Stiles and Little would interview him nevertheless.

The California Corrections Institution for Men was a medium security prison in Chino, where Melvin Ripinski was incarcerated. Ripinski was brought to a holding cell where he was shackled to a bench that was buried in the concrete slab. He resembled James in a cursory way. He was young, muscled and inked up and down both arms. His eyes were a tired blue-gray and his skull was dirty white from the prison buzz cut.

He looked at Traci and grinned. "You come to parole me, right?"

"I'm afraid not, Melvin," she said. "We want some info about your relatives. We've already met James. Who else you got?"

"I ain't got nobody more but Luke. That fuckwad step in the shit again?"

Stiles said, "We really don't know yet. Is he younger or older than you?"

"Luke's younger by two years. Me and James been havin' trouble with him since he was a zygote. He's got a sheet a yard long."

"What's his problem?" Traci asked.

"Women." He looked her up and down. "Speakin' of which, your ass is the best I seen all day."

"Thanks, enjoy it while you can."

Stiles got to the point. "Okay, so where is Luke living these days?"

"Hollywood. He's got a pad on Virgil. 607 North, second floor."

"Thanks. We'll say hello."

"Better be careful, I was you. He's got a Baby Browning . 25 strapped to his leg."

"Thanks for the tip."

"Do I get anything outta this?"

"Maybe it's worth a word to the Parole Board."

"I can use that, man."

Stiles and Traci met with two patrol units a block down Virgil from Luke Ripinski's rundown apartment building and advanced by foot. Silently they closed in on the entrance. Two officers ascended the stairs with Stiles and Little right behind, and edged down the faded hallway room 205. There was no response to the P/Os' pounding and shouts of POLICE! OPEN UP! After a ten second pause, they used a battering ram to break the lock. Inside they saw Luke Ripinski bailing out of a window onto a fire escape. No matter, he faced the drawn guns of two patrol cops. One cuffed Luke before he could even find his ankle. Luke wasn't exactly happy about it.

"Fuckin' weenie-sucker cops," he screeched. "Ow! That hurts."

John Luttwak took Diane out to a restaurant. A real one, not the Full Clip. Seated at their window booth they had a nice view of Marina del Rey, and a sailboat idling in to dock no more than fifty feet away. He ordered two glasses of chardonnay. His normal inclination would be to a red, but this was to please Diane.

Outside, a night heron swooped in to alight on the top of the sailboat's mast. They'd seen the same bird several times before perching on the masts or walking back and forth on the dock, looking in the murky water for the movements of small crabs. This time Luttwak made no comment.

Diane could sense his moods like a Dalmatian. She smiled for him and said, "What's got into you tonight, hon?"

He placed a letter on the table. "I've been offered the position of Security Supervisor for Interstate Energy Corporation."

"Really. Right out of the blue sky."

"Yeah." He laughed at his own expense. "I guess somebody's trying to get rid of me."

"Nonsense. They heard about you from some trendy head hunter outfit."

"Maybe so. Whatever, I thought I'd seek your professional counsel."

"Hm, this sounds serious."

"Well, it pays almost twice what I get now, plus a very good retirement plan."

"You already have a good retirement plan."

Ignoring that, Luttwak went on, "And I get a corner office at their headquarters with a view of the grounds."

"While sitting at a desk in Parched Creek, Arizona, reciting Ditat Deus."

"What's that?"

Another smile. "The state motto. God enriches."

"So I take it you're not in favor."

"No, darling, *you* are not in favor. You'd go totally apeshit in a job like that. No more action, no more putting away gangsters and rapists. No more teams of terrific detectives. No more being crucial. Because that's exactly what you are, you know."

"Thanks, sweetheart. I was going to turn it down, but I just wanted to make sure."

The wine came and they clinked glasses. "You want to go see a movie after?"

"No, I want to go home and get personal with you."

32

Luke Ripinski was borderline handsome, 6-foot 1-inch, 220 pounds, all of it shackled to the bench. His blonde buzz cut and vacant blue eyes were just like his brother's.

Stiles and Little came into the room and plopped their papers down. Stiles turned on the tape machine. Luke looked at him and said, "I see there's at least two white cops in the LAPD."

"You want to elaborate on that?" Stiles said.

"You can't touch me. All the liberal weepy hearts around here seen to that."

"Never mind. You want a soda?"

"Yeah. Lemon."

Stiles exited the room and spoke to an officer.

"So where were you at 10: 30 last Monday night?" Traci said to Ripinski.

"I don't know. Where were you?"

"That's about the time when Fauna Corbyn was stabbed to death."

"Who's she?"

"The woman you were raping at the time."

Luke Ripinski snickered. "You can't prove that because I wasn't there."

"Or maybe you're impotent. Can't get it up, Luke?"

"Unzip me, honey, and see for yourself."

Stiles was back with two sodas and two foam cups. He handed a soda to Traci and one to Ripinski. "Courtesy of the LAPD," he said.

"Stupid styrofoam," Ripinski said. "I'll drink from the can."

"Let's get back to business," Stiles said. "You ever been in the military, Luke?"

"Go find out."

"Ever skinned a rabbit?"

"Rabbit meat sucks."

"Enough of your bullshit. What if we told you we have incontrovertible evidence that you were there, namely that your prints were on the knife."

"I would've used gloves, stupid."

"Only you didn't, right?"

"Why don't you fuckers get me a free lawyer, like the weepy hearts want."

"You're gonna need one, Luke. In the meantime we'll give you free room and board."

"Shit, you got nothin' and you know it."

"Just keep digging your hole. You're almost there."

Stiles slid his chair back and went to the door. "Officer, get this puke out of my sight."

After Ripinski was gone, Stiles bagged the soda can for Trace Analysis Unit. Ten days later a report showed up via E-mail. The DNA from the knife and the can were a perfect match. Luke was going to be off the streets for life.

Late afternoon Saturday, Stiles and Traci were lying side by side on her roof again. The sky was a cloudless robin's egg blue.

"Did you hear about John Luttwak's offer from Interstate Energy?" Traci said.

"Yeah, I did. But don't worry, he won't take it."

"It's pretty lucrative, I hear."

"Wak's not the sort of man that goes for lucre. He needs the LAPD, and the LAPD needs him. It's a perfect fit."

A beating in the air increased as two Police choppers passed overhead.

"You ever think about retirement?"

"No. When the time comes I'll handle it, thank you very much."

"I think about us a lot. What'll happen when I get old and baggy?"

"You'll get old, but never baggy. It's not in your genes."

"You been poking around in my genes again?"

"Yes. I've looked everywhere, but I can't find 'em."

"Speaking of looks, you were totally eating up Kim Kaelin the other day."

"She's criminally gorgeous. As gorgeous as you, only not you."

"Okay, I'll settle for that."

"You know, what pisses me off is that we can't go on a date like regular people. I'd love to take you to an actual restaurant, or to a movie, or to a ball game. Without worrying about McKnight's spies on our tail."

"I know. We've gone out like two entire times. Maybe we should throw caution to the wind and just let it happen. What do you think?"

"Hey, I'm willing if you are."

"If we get caught, we can always quit and open our own Agency."

"There you go. Stiles and Little Investigations."

"No, Little and Stiles Investigations."

"You're a real smart ass today, aren't you."

They were silent for a while, just lying there catching the late rays.

The grit and gristle of the streets was fading and Stiles was at peace for a change. Unused to such serenity, it felt unnatural to him. At length he said, "I don't know what will become of Traci, but whatever it is, I want you beside me."

Traci was amazed. "What's got into you, Jack? That's th sweetest thing you've ever said to me."

"Better get used to it, girl."

She gave him a poke. "Get on your back, detective. I want to check your tensor fasciae latae."

Luttwak lay awake, at the mercy of his thoughts. He never really expected Diane would want him to take that offer. He simply felt it was a decision for two to make. They both had deep roots at the LAPD. At Hollywood Division in particular, where their colleagues were like family.

Tomorrow he would look out the window of his office and see all those black and whites lined up in the lot, waiting to be checked out. Patrol units ready to go forth into roiling, sun-blazing Los Angeles to protect the people, just like it says on the cruisers' doors. Ready to respond to bloody crime scenes, chase down rapists, break up gang fights, and come to the aid of ladies having their purses snatched in dark parking lots. Ready to help addled old men find their way home.

It was stressful, frustrating, often dangerous work. Sometimes a fire fight would break out and brave men and women would fall. That's what a cop could expect in line of duty, Luttwak knew. And yet the faith and dedication was still there in remarkable strength.

It had been a difficult year for Luttwak. He thought of Carina, the beautiful Latina in the bloom of life, wasted like a bag of stale tortillas. And Charlie Telford, a decent cop shot down in the street and left for dead. He must call Stella, he reminded himself. And now Fauna Corbyn, slain in the most obscene way. He wondered what further horrors awaited as the year's clock wound down.

us,

urs, Luttwak's phone chirped. He reached across
ed Diane to pick up. The call was no great surprise.
nt Watch Captain, alerting him to another incidence
e crime. Again, somewhere in beautiful Hollywood,
ere not far from its famous boulevard of inlaid stars, the
s and the gangsters and the killers were coming out to work
r evil in the night.

So be it, Luttwak thought. L.A. was still the town he loved
and cherished and it always would be. He would fight for it until
he could fight no longer and others would come to fight on after
him. The city was strong, he knew, as strong as the people who
lived in it. And the people would prevail.

ABOUT THE AUTHOR

Roger F. Kennedy writes mainly of Southern California.
His background is in design and the arts. He was
art director of a Los Angeles advertising agency and later
operated a graphic design studio, where he received many
awards for graphic excellence.
He now lives in a Southland coastal community with
his wife Lois and their black cat Poco.

Edwards Brothers, Inc.
Thorofare, NJ USA
July 14, 2011